Saturday Stories

Celebrating
30 Years of Publishing
in India

Saturday Stories

RASHMI BANSAL

HarperCollins *Publishers* India

First published in India by HarperCollins *Publishers* 2023
4th Floor, Tower A, Building No. 10, DLF Cyber City,
DLF Phase II, Gurugram, Haryana – 122002
www.harpercollins.co.in

2 4 6 8 10 9 7 5 3 1

Copyright © Rashmi Bansal 2023

P-ISBN: 978-93-5699-307-5
E-ISBN: 978-93-5699-311-2

This is a work of fiction and all characters and incidents described in this book are the product of the authors' imagination. Any resemblance to actual persons, living or dead, is entirely coincidental.

Rashmi Bansal asserts the moral right
to be identified as the author of this work.

All rights reserved. No part of this publication may be reproduced, stored in a retrieval system, or transmitted, in any form or by any means, electronic, mechanical, photocopying, recording or otherwise, without the prior permission of the publishers.

Typeset in 11.5/15.5 Adobe garamond at
Manipal Technologies Limited, Manipal

Printed and bound at
Thomson Press (India) Ltd

This book is produced from independently certified FSC® paper
to ensure responsible forest management.

*Dedicated to Lata,
because behind every successful woman stands
another woman.*

A blue Kanjeevaram sari, stained with sorrow.
A cycle pedalled furiously, while dreaming of tomorrow.
We know not how this life will unfold –
That's the theme of this book you hold.

Contents

Free at Last	1
What They Don't Teach You at Harvard Business School	4
How I Met Your Mother	7
Grapes of Rot	12
Diamonds Are Forever	16
Ode to Love	20
Lambi Race ki Ghodi	25
Lord of the Rings	29
The Last Tribe	33
Hum Aapke Hain Kaun	37
Child's Play	40
A Woman of Substance	44
State of Mind	48
Chal Meri Dhanno	52
Taking a Chance	56
Real Medicine	60
Faking It	64
A Matter of Pride	68

Main Shayar toh Nahin	72
Think Pink	75
Path of Destiny	79
Memories of Midnight	83
Mistress of Spices	87
Stand by Me	91
Rishtey Naatey	95
Work Is Worship	99
Tell Me Why	103
Bachpan ke Din	107
Mission Impossible	111

Scan the QR code at the end of each story for an audio bite from the author

Workshop Stories
(By students of Rashmi Bansal's short-story writing programme)

And That's the Way the Cookie Crumbled	117
The Witness	122
Till We Meet Again	127
Flying High	132
Free to Be Me	138
Ammaji	145
A Note from the Author	155
Acknowledgements	157

Free at Last

The park bench is rough. I run my fingers up and down the wood, and feel a splinter trying to get under my skin. Ah! I feel alive.

In my hand is an apple. Red, round, shiny. I take a bite and chew slowly, very slowly. The juice spreads in my mouth, trickles down my throat. This is bliss.

The sun is in the sky and its light is falling on my face. On my arms, my legs, every exposed part of my body. My mind doesn't say, 'It's hot.' It just says, 'How wonderful.'

After thirty months of lockdown, I am finally 'free'. They said it was a 'temporary measure' to contain the virus. The first twenty-one days were kind of nice – a break from normal life.

But then they lifted it and within two weeks the virus was back with a vengeance. So we had another lockdown, and then another, and yet another. Until we lost track of time.

What day of the week is it anyway? Don't know.

What do we wake up and do each morning? Don't know.

When will this nightmare end? Don't know.

We tried keeping ourselves busy, of course. Taking online classes for everything. Learning new recipes. Catching up with old friends on Zoom and Skype.

But I missed normal life. The routine, the humdrum of every day – things I took for granted. Oh, what I would have given to just walk out of home and buy bread from the corner shop.

I was one of the lucky ones, I know. Who went to sleep at night on a full stomach. Across the world, people were succumbing to hunger and disease.

Social security, government grants and doles were not enough. For man does not live to eat alone. Isolated, stripped of freedom, starved of hope, the human race lost its humanity.

We became statistics in the news – X infected, Y dead, Z recovered.

For months, scientists were working on a vaccine. It took much longer than expected. Finally, twenty-six months into the lockdown, they made the grand announcement.

'We are all saved.'

Well, not 'all', of course. The vaccine does not come cheap. And there is limited production. So you must be able to pay for it and be lucky enough to receive it.

It's what you might call a game of Human Roulette.

I am one of the Chosen Few. A jab in the arm and two days of fever was what it cost. And now my mobile phone flashes 'green' when I walk out of my apartment.

I can buy bread from the corner shop, but, sadly, the corner shop is closed. So is the barber, the baker, the furniture-maker. Out of business or out of this world altogether, I wonder.

And so I sit on a park bench and cherish the moment. In a way I never ever did before. I wish there were children and grandparents and lovers on the grass. Maybe someday.

Ah, what a glorious day!

I am waiting to be assigned a task in service of the nation. Or, I should say, the world. For the only way to fight this virus is to dissolve our differences. And come together as One.

***

In a galaxy far, far away: Alpha to Beta, Alpha to Beta, 'Do you copy?'

Beta to Alpha, 'Copy. Trial successful ... 41,672 Homo sapiens implanted with the controller chip via vaccine.'

Colonization is really that simple.

What They Don't Teach You at Harvard Business School

Like every other business in the world, Champak's little enterprise had been wiped out by Covid-19. Since the lockdown was put in place – over a month ago – he had been sitting at home, twiddling his thumbs.

The team of ustads painstakingly groomed and trained by him, was also sitting at home, watching porn on their mobile phones while claiming to watch *Ramayan*.

'Bhai, aisi mandi toh aaj tak dekhi nahin …' Champak muttered to himself, while trying to swallow the nth meal of dal and rice made by his wife. She was looking increasingly harassed day by day.

'Kya hai yeh virus ... Sab ko pareshaan kar rakha hai,' she wailed to her sister in Jhansi at least three times a day on video call. She had eaten away at Champak's brains for breakfast, lunch, dinner and midnight snacks before he finally agreed to get her an iPhone. His condition was, 'yeh phone ab paanch saal chalaana padega'.

That Chanda could live with. She had never clamoured for a fancy apartment or car, content to live in a chawl in south Mumbai. The building didn't even have a lift. Champak had warned her before their marriage that she would be well provided for. But, in his line of work, it was best to keep a low profile. So no jazz and no showing off ... Simple hi rehna padega.

This suited Chanda just fine. She had grown up in a chawl herself, and enjoyed the bonhomie that came with open windows and shared toilets. They had managed to bring up three daughters here, married them off well (the only time Champak did show off a little). And now, it was just the two of them – no health problems, no wealth problems. Insaan ko aur kya chahiye?

'Bas ek cheez, ek cheez chahiye,' Chanda burst out one morning before dissolving into tears. 'Mujhe hair dye ka ek dabba chahiye.'

Champak looked at his wife – *really* looked at her – and saw a middle-aged woman with crazed eyes and a swathe of safed baal peeking out of her scalp. Like wheat standing tall in the fields, this patch was crying out to be sprayed with chemicals. Champak felt a wave of sympathy for Chanda. Yes, yes, of course, it was his duty as a husband.

That's when a light bulb went off in Champaklal's head. Business is all about demand and supply.

This was not the time to buy jewellery or mobile phones – the two items that used to be his bread and butter. In fact, *butter* was the thing to procure, buyer toh mil hi jayega.

Champak called his ustads on WhatsApp and conveyed the good news. There would be a strategic shift in the line of business. But modus operandi would remain the same. Night shift would be mandatory, wearing masks and gloves would not be an issue. They were already well versed with its benefits.

Two days later, Chanda got her Most Wanted Item and was in seventh heaven. She now video calls her sister six times a day, just to make her jealous.

***

Champak's diversification strategy paid off. In fact, it even got covered in the *Times of India* this morning: 'A string of burglaries has been reported from kirana stores in the suburbs of Mumbai. Among the items taken were 200 packets of Maggi noodles, 100 sticks of Amul butter and 50 packs of Godrej Natural Black hair dye …'

How I Met Your Mother

Kids, I know you are bored with this lockdown. Well, you know what people did in the old days, when there was no TV, no internet, no Instagram or Snapchat? They told stories.

They sat around a tree and told stories. They sat around the fire and told stories. So now, let me tell you a story.

Is it a true story? Well, that's for you to decide. I am just the storyteller.

Once upon a time, there was a handsome young man called Ted. He was born in Poughkeepsie, NY, to a father who was a dentist and a mother who was a homemaker. He lived in a house with a white picket fence, a tricycle in the garden and the smell of cinnamon rolls wafting from the kitchen.

It was a happy childhood. He was a good student. There was just one problem. Ted could never fall in love. Well, he did fall for a lot of girls, but they never knew that. Because he never mustered the courage to say those three magic words.

But Mr Nice Guy lost out to the Studs and the Sweet-Talkers. The kind who broke young girls' hearts as if they were cheap bottles of wine. Some of them came and cried on Ted's strong shoulders. But he was too nice to take advantage of the situation.

(Prompting one girl to say, years later, 'You know, all men are not Harvey Weinsteins.')

Well, Ted excelled at everything academic and went on to Harvard Business School. There, he met a guy called Ram (short for Ramanamurty Kondapalli Sivapillai Mohanram). Ram was as bad as Ted in the 'getting a girlfriend' department.

But Ram had one significant advantage: A mom who was on the prowl. You see, India has this system of 'arranged marriage', where your parents find you a suitable match. This system has saved thousands – nay, millions – of bespectacled, bewildered becharas, otherwise known as nerds.

When Ram completed his studies and returned to India, there was a gal waiting to walk around the holy fire with him. And become the joint holder of his plump HDFC bank account. Ted ... Poor, poor Ted. He attended the ceremony and cursed his luck.

If only he had been born in beautiful, backward, brides-aplenty India.

A cousin of Ram's noticed the lost-looking angrez and decided to have some fun with the chap.

'Hey ... Why so sad on this happy occasion, mate?' said Cousin in a Tam-Tex drawl.

Ted did not reply, but what else could a young man at a wedding be sad about?

'Okay, brother, you wanna know when *you* will get married? Show me your hand ...'

Tam-Tex was now squinting at an outstretched palm with all the concentration he generally used to stare at the lizard on his wall.

'The Heart Line is in collision with the Head Line ... Ohoho ... Difficult, but not impossible ...'

And then he scrunched up his eyes and said, 'I see a window ... You are standing near a window ... You will see her from a window.'

And that was that was that.

On the plane back to New York, Ted kept staring out of his window. Would the woman of his dreams appear outside of it? Nah ... Humbug! These crazy Indians, full of superstitions.

But from that moment on, he simply could not stop staring out of windows. Bus windows, car windows, home windows, office windows, shop windows ... And if nothing, there was always Microsoft Windows.

Well, that was the window which led him to date and Emate, Soulmate.com and Hotplate.porn. He met girls and made out with them, but ... it was not the real thing. There was no spark, no ignition of the heart.

'Oh, you are a hopeless romantic,' said his sister, who had married her high-school sweetheart.

On his thirtieth birthday, Ted's family gave him a surprise: A trip to Italy. It was a welcome break! Rome, Florence, Venice, Pisa ... So wrapped up was our man in the sights and smells of *la dolce tourisme*, he missed a very, very important piece of news.

And thus, the lockdown caught him completely by surprise. He was trapped in fair Verona, in an Airbnb, with no friends, no family and very little food. While one can live on bread, butter and bananas alone ... suddenly one morning, a soul-stirring piece of music tickled his ear.

Where? How?

He rushed to the window and right opposite him, an ethereal creature was playing the violin in her balcony. It was a moment in time, one to be cherished forever. Faithfully recorded on his Apple XR, shared on social media, re-shared a million times the world over.

'The glorious spirit of Italy, of humanity – see it in wine and song pouring out of its balconies!'

But who *was* that girl? A fair maiden who could use a knight in a shining mask to fetch her groceries. But how would he reach out to her? Wave from his window? Shout across the road? What if she thought he was a madman ...?

Ted cursed his luck, his life, his loser genes and the bloody lockdown.

***

The next morning

A message on Instagram from 'Belladonna': 'I'm the girl you filmed last night. You've made me famous! Come to your window, I'll play a song for you!!'

The arrow of Eros struck the violinist the moment she saw sweet Signor Ted. She serenaded him for hours ... He sent her virtual kisses and flowers.

And, kids, THAT is how I met your mother.

Grapes of Rot

THE AIR WAS FRAGRANT WITH PROMISE. LIKE A WOMAN IN the final days of her pregnancy, the grapes on the vine were oh-so plump. In a day or two, they would be ready to harvest.

At this time of the year, Dhondu would be in seventh heaven. His fortunes had skyrocketed ever since had switched to growing grapes. It wasn't easy in the beginning, but once he got the hang of it, there was no looking back. From a modest 1 acre, his farm had now expanded to 10. Ghar pe aaya television, two motorcycles, solar panels, and the latest addition – a computer.

'*Kaytari naveen karnaar faydecha aahe* (Doing new things brings rewards),' he would boast to his friends and relatives, who were still cultivating jowari or wheat.

But this year, he sat on the charpoy in his verandah with his head in his hands. Some strange disease called 'corona' had gripped the country. The mandi was shut, transport suspended and all the workers had disappeared. So how was he going to harvest the grapes and where the hell would he sell them? The future was looking bleak …

In despair, Dhondu summoned his three sons and asked, 'Do you have some new idea … Something that can get us out of this mess?'

The oldest of the three, Vilas, was a hefty young man with a bit of a swagger. He had heard of something called 'wine' made from grapes.

'Baba, *aamhi* try *karto, angooracha daru tayar karto …*'

Making wine? At any other time, Dhondu would have rapped the boy's knuckles. But desperate times call for desperate measures. He gave him the green signal.

'Take 3 acres of grapes … But do something!'

The second son, Ulhas, was more practical. He knew of someone with a chikoo farm, who had loaded a tempo and sold his harvest in Mumbai. Not in the wholesale market, but directly to customers. The chikoo farmer sent out a WhatsApp message, offering the fruit at an attractive price to any housing society willing to place a bulk order.

In this way he had sold over 600 kg of chikoo in a single day. Dhondu was not fully convinced, but he gave Ulhas the green signal too.

'Take 6 acres of grapes ... But do it quickly!'

Ulhas was a clever chap and even came up with a scheme to procure labour. He called the district collector and got information about the nearest migrant workers' camp. As harvesting is an 'essential service', he managed to get eight labourers to pick the grapes. They were housed in a makeshift tent under the shade of a banyan tree, with aai's kitchen supplying bajre ki roti, poli and chaha.

Thanks to the wonders of WhatsApp, orders started coming in. Hiring a tempo at double the price, Ulhas made a dash to Mumbai and managed to sell most of the grapes. It didn't yield a huge profit, but was enough to raise Dhondu's spirits. He would not have to worry about money for the next few months.

But what was still worrying him was his youngest son, Ninad. An acre of grapes remained to be picked. When he tried to get Ninad to take responsibility for it, the boy was indifferent.

'Baba, *majhi* online class *madhe* disturb *nako kara*. Let the grapes be as they are.'

Ever since Ninad had enrolled in the agricultural university in Nagpur, his head was in the clouds. He kept talking about strange new things he had learnt of, which made no sense to Dhondu. And now that he was back home from the hostel, all he did was talk to the computer. Who talks to a computer!

Why, even that useless Vilas had tried to help at least!

Wine bana nahi ... because it was not that easy. But it had been enjoyable for him to jump on all those grapes. Thoda tension body se nikal gaya.

If only Ninad would realize – a farmer's son must think like a farmer. Damn this education!

***

Six weeks later, the grapes on that last acre had transformed into 'raisins on the vine'. Plump, juicy and sold for five times the price of ordinary grapes.

'Baba, my professor was guiding me step-by-step. Thank him! And thank the computer ...'

Now, all the farmers in the area are queuing outside Dhondu's door to learn how to make raisins on the vine.

Kaytari naveen shiknaar faydecha hote! (Learning new things brings rewards!)

Diamonds Are Forever

Meghji Damjibhai Shah was a worried man. As chairman of the Surat Diamond Merchant's Association, he had faced many tough situations. In any industry, there were always disputes. Between members, with the labour, and sometimes with clients. Meghji had one simple principle in life, which had always served him well.

'Vyaapar se badhkar vyavhaar'. How you treat people is more important than money.

His mind went back to his first benefactor – a distant uncle, who had visited his native village. Laljibhai was running a small diamond polishing unit; a new business which was growing fast. He offered sixteen-year-old Meghji a job as an apprentice. The boy was thrilled to move to Surat, where life offered many more opportunities compared to Amreli.

Meghji was a quick learner and was determined to become an ace diamond cutter. In a year's time, he was earning Rs 1,000 per month, most of which he sent home to support the family and pay off long-standing debts. And that was why when his mother brought up the topic of marriage, he was hesitant. Would his wife be willing to live this frugal a life in the big city?

Rakshaben was just the life partner he was hoping for. Not only did she manage the house on his small income, she decided to supplement it as well. As a girl, Raksha had mastered the art of papad-making, which few in the city had time for. She started a small business and, as demand grew, soon enlisted the ladies in the neighbourhood to join her.

A couple of years later, Laljibhai decided to send his nephew to Antwerp. It was an alien world, dealing with the Jewish traders who controlled the diamond business. They did not take kindly to these strange new Indians entering their territory. But the Palanpuri Jains were clever. They picked the smallest diamonds, which no one was willing to cut and polish.

'Give us a chance to show what is possible,' said Meghji to prospective buyers in broken English.

One day, Meghji went to show some samples to Rosnovski & Co., one of the biggest in the business. The owner himself inspected a few stones. As he peered through the powerful magnifying glass, Mr Rosnovski snorted and pointed out a flaw. Meghji offered to re-examine each and every stone, and bring a perfect lot the next morning. A painstaking job which took all night.

Impressed by the young man's attitude, Rosnovski became a trusted client. A few years later, with the blessings (and some capital) from his uncle, Meghji set up his own company. Now, he was running a Rs 5,000-crore empire with the help of his brothers, sons and 3,500 employees, all of whom Meghji considered as 'family'. Raksha Gems had offices in Antwerp, Mumbai and London.

But, since the last two months, everything had come to a standstill. Coronavirus had shut not just his factory, but all industries in Surat. More than 10 lakh migrant workers were now jobless, and struggling to get two square meals a day. Meghjibhai appealed to the diamond merchant community to open their hearts and their pockets, to donate generously to the cause.

And more than Rs 10 crore were thus collected. A community kitchen was set up and Meghji was personally supervising operations. But they were now facing an unexpected problem.

Working in the hot kitchen in the summer heat was a nightmare. There were not enough tawas, not enough cooks … When he confided in Rakshaben, she simply laughed.

'Finally you men are understanding what it's like to work in the kitchen.'

With lightning speed, she sent out a message on various WhatsApp groups. Surely, this would strike a chord …

***

Two weeks later

Barkha Dutt reports on a unique model of community kitchen which has taken over Surat, supplying over 1,50,000 hot and fresh chapatis daily.

'Every housewife in the city is making five extra chapatis to feed migrant workers. I am with Rakshaben, who is masterminding this "work from home" effort …'

Meghji had never been prouder of his wife. For the brightest gems are not in any factory, but right here, in our homes.

Ode to Love

Act 1

There was a city, Verona,
Struck by the virus corona.
Famous for Romeo and Juliet,
The families Montague and Capulet,
Had they lived happily ever after,
With grandchildren, music and laughter,
Tourists would not visit the city
Throw coins into fountains so pretty.
For lost love is the most romantic,
Untainted by life and its antics,

Now 400 years have passed in Verona,
Suffering from virus corona,
A boy stands on his balcony,
Feeling all sad and melancholy.
The country is under a lockdown,
The city is now but a ghost town,
People are holed up in houses
With kids and insufferable spouses.
And some, like him, are alone,
Their only companion, the phone,
Surviving on boiled rice and pasta,
And that too until it will last-a.
So imagine the surprise and joy,
To see a beautiful young lady so coy,
In a balcony across the street,
Playing the violin so sweet.

Act 2

Struck by the arrow of Cupid,
The one that makes people real stupid,
I must know thy name, bella donna,
More importantly, your online persona.
For I am not as agile as Romeo,
Who climbed up to meet his lady-o,
And why would I do that, madam,
When she must be on Instagram.
A search bar supplied all the info,

All I did was send out an intro.
Then she replied in a jiffy,
We chatted and flirted till dizzy,
The love-talk went on through the week,
She taught me to cook, I sang her to sleep,
Virtual kisses were exchanged on Skype,
(and some naughtier stuff we will not write).
Two weeks after the concert on the balcony,
Two hearts were thinking of matrimony.
The boy decided to make a proposal,
Such that there was no chance of refusal.
A giant red heart and a Bluetooth speaker,
Conveyed his desire to keep her.
In the presence of neighbours and friends,
The balcony proposal happily ends.
They cheer and clap and throw confetti,
The video goes viral in every country,
Good news is rare in a pandemic,
Love in a lockdown is epic.
The lovers will kiss for an hour,
Once Covid has lost all its power.
In the fair city of Verona,
Struck by the virus of corona,
Will love survive reality,
Routine and human frailty?
Stay tuned for the tale to unfold,
Season 1 rights have been sold.

Act 3

In the long run I suspect,
Corona will lose its effect.
That Cupid guy is more stealthy,
Striking the young and the healthy,
Making us all believe in magic,
And then … revealing the tragic.
We all need a whole lot of space,
But we need to survive as a race.
So we end up staying with spouses,
Yet stare into opposite houses,
Wondering if they are any happier,
Are their love lives sweeter and sappier?
I want one Mr William Shakespeare,
To discuss this over a beer.
Please clarify for the good of humanity,
Is love merely a form of insanity?
I'm quite sure my heart will not waver,
When, dear Juliet, you are a cadaver.
How do we learn to love and to cherish,
When we live on and refuse to perish,
Stuck with the same guy for fifty years,
The thought makes me burst into tears.

Finale

Far from the fair city of Verona,
During the time of virus corona,
I look at my parents, and I realize,
'Love' is right in front of my eyes.
The kind which is quiet, consistent and real,
Not in a movie, not a big deal.
To the couple a balcony apart,
I wish you a lasting affair of the heart.
May your marriage not feel like forced quarantine,
May you age together like a bottle of wine,
Wherever in the world you may be now,
Long after defeating corona.

Lambi Race ki Ghodi

๑

Visiting the supermarket was one of the small pleasures in Mona's life. Sure, she was a super-qualified, over-achieving professional. The kind who could buckle down and work thirty-six hours at a stretch. But, in her heart of hearts, she was a homebody who loved to poke her nose into the fridge and decide what to cook for dinner.

Unlike so many of her friends, Mona did not have a husband or kids to cater to. And she had no regrets about that. She had been briefly married in her twenties, and it had lasted just two years. The lack of a 'family' didn't really bother Mona, and it gave her the flexibility to do things which other women could not.

Like picking up her suitcase and shifting to a whole new country, where she had an amazing opportunity to work at a high-tech company.

'There is no future in this country,' she said to her girlfriends over drinks just before leaving.

It was a sixteen-hour flight with a longish stopover in London. Mona wasn't worse for wear, having flown business class. At arrivals, the immigration process was quick and painless. As she wheeled out her luggage, everything appeared shiny and new. What a contrast to the tired old airport of her hometown. A high-speed freeway took her straight into the city.

Her new colleagues were welcoming and she quickly settled in. After two weeks in a hotel, she found a nice, furnished apartment.

'I love it here!' she said to her mother when they spoke. 'I feel right at home!'

One of Mona's worries while travelling had been how to manage her dietary needs. When she became a vegan ten years ago, her mom was shocked. Maybe one could manage without eating meat, but what about milk, cheese and butter? It sounded quite unwise and unhealthy. But Mona had proven her wrong. She was fit and fine at forty-one, active and alert.

Yes, it meant one could not eat out as much, but that was a small price to pay. This was also why Mona loved supermarkets. Almost any dish could be made vegan if you cooked it with your own hands. And the supermarket she had encountered, not far from her new apartment, was absolutely to die for.

Never had Mona seen such a variety of fruits and vegetables, aisles and aisles of amazing foods and superfoods. And great prices, too.

Well, just when Mona was thinking about how lucky she was, her life was turned upside down. By the lockdown. Sure, there had been news reports about some virus spreading in China, but it all seemed like it was happening so far away. Until, all of a sudden, it was at your doorstep. One day it was 'just two cases', a few days later, it was 'getting out of hand'.

'Work from home,' was the terse instruction from the office.

'Jump onto a plane and come back!' her mother had implored her. But it was too late. Flights had been suspended, and no one knew when they would restart.

'Well, at least I must stock up on groceries,' she thought. And headed out with a long list in hand.

As expected, there was a queue outside the store, and only a handful of shoppers were allowed inside at a time. After a half-hour wait, when it was finally Mona's turn, she was in for a shock.

The guard shouted a racial slur and blocked her way. The shoppers behind her nodded in agreement.

'Go back home, you dirty foreigner,' they yelled, 'We don't want you here.'

Tears pricked Mona's eyes. She had heard of xenophobia, but never experienced it. How small and powerless she felt in that moment.

How unwanted.

***

The next morning, American citizen Mona Williams received a call from the police commissioner of Hyderabad city.

'Madam, we are very, very sorry to hear about this incident. There is a rumour that foreigners are spreading the coronavirus ... So people are scared ... It is very wrong.'

Mona sighed ... Was this payback from the Universe? A world where White is the new Black.

Lord of the Rings

🕉

It was a moonless night in the month of March when the Hebbars were awakened by an eerie sound. The first to hear it was Aishwarya. She leapt out of bed and rushed to granny's room.

'Pati!' the six-year-old sobbed, clinging to the old lady's sari. 'There is a bhoot in the house ...'

The commotion had woken up the girl's parents.

'What? Ghost? What books are you reading before you sleep, magu?' admonished her mother.

Purnima Hebbar was quite tired with the exertions of the day. Cooking was an endless activity ... And more so during this season. One day, there was a ton of raw mango to be pickled; another day, a mountain of coconuts to make chutney out of. Tomorrow, there would be some guests at lunchtime.

'You go back to sleep,' said Pati, with a wave of her hand. 'Aishu will sleep with me today.'

At that very moment, the shrill laughter of a child filled the humid night air. A chill ran down Purnima's spine. This was not someone's overactive imagination. This was real.

The sound grew louder and shriller. It was not coming from inside the house, though.

'Let me find out what this is,' said Mr Hebbar with convincing bravado. At the door, he picked up a lathi which once belonged to his father. His sweaty palms made it difficult for him to get a grip.

It was a sprawling bungalow with typical red Mangalore tiles, a large garden and a small plantation. This was where Prakash had grown up; he knew it like the back of his hand.

But that night, everything seemed different. As he made his way around the perimeter, Prakash almost expected to bump into a ghostly apparition. The combined effect of all the horror films he had watched – to hold hands with various girls in college – came rushing to his mind. In full technicolour and Dolby Stereo sound.

The eerie laughter floated towards him again, mocking the fully grown man. Prakash followed the high-pitched sound until he found himself near a coconut tree. This was where the sinister chortling was coming from. Of that, he was quite sure. He stood there for some time, breathing heavily. But the 'bhoot' had decided to call it a day.

Nobody slept that night. The next morning, Purnima should have been busy preparing a feast for their guests. But she hastily prepared only a simple bisi bele bhaat. Right away, her aunt and uncle knew something was wrong. Reluctantly, Prakash related the incident to them, wondering if it was at all believable …

'Such a small thing,' said Kaka. 'Here, call this fellow and he will solve your problem.'

A few hours later, a man with a long beard, flowing locks and a chain of plastic skulls around his neck, arrived. He circled the tree, muttering something to himself. Then he threw some cowrie shells at it.

'I knew it! A spirit is trapped in the tree … Don't worry. I have handled hundreds of such cases.'

Naturally, this handling came at a cost. After brisk negotiations, the exorcist agreed to perform a ceremony to get rid of the spirit. For just 25,000 rupees.

The sun had just set that evening, night was falling, when all of a sudden, they were startled out of their skins. The eerie sound of a child, laughing like a banshee. Deva, when will this nightmare end!

***

As they huddled inside the house, a wiry young man entered the compound and headed straight for the tree. He clambered up like a monkey and slithered down a few minutes later. With a plastic pouch in hand and a wide grin on his face.

'Sister,' he said to a startled Purnima. 'When I came to remove your coconuts the other day, I left my mobile up there! Every night I am calling, calling, but no reply!'

The Last Tribe

Deep in the jungles of Bastar, a young tribal woman goes about her morning chores. She is barefoot, dressed in a soft cotton sari which lightly covers her breasts.

Like the ladies in lockdown are discovering, life is really so free without a bra.

Basa heads into the forest with a basket fashioned from bamboo leaves. Here, far from civilization, there are no grocery shops selling atta and dal, packaged food or water. You eat what the forest provides – fruit, shoots, herbs, leaves and eggs. On most days, Nature is generous. There is enough – and more – to keep the stomach satisfied.

She heads back to the village, humming a Gondi tune under her breath. Her four-year-old son and two-year-old daughter are awake and playing outside the hut.

'Wait, my child, I will prepare food for you,' she says, tenderly scooping up the toddler in her arms.

Basa opens the storeroom to bring out some firewood. This is a recent addition to her modest home. A year ago, some government contractor came and did a survey. They built a room with a hole in the ground for every home in the village. They said it was a 'toilet'. But why should anyone go to the toilet inside a room when they have the vast, open jungle for the same purpose?

The young mother prepares a gruel of kodo millet and some paste from the green leafy vegetables she collected that morning. Tired with the exertions of the day, she takes a swig from a small earthen jar. The liquid penetrates her throat and warmth spreads throughout her body. As a drowsy feeling sweeps over her, she lies down on the cool mud floor.

In her dream world, Basa is a little girl, helping her mother in the forest.

'Look what I found,' her mother exclaims with excitement. There, in the leaves of the sal tree, were ingredients for a chutney they all relished. The older woman carefully collects as much as she can carry and hurries back. She pounds the chapda with a mortar and pestle, adds chili and salt, and tastes it.

Mmm … just the right amount of zing.

Someone is at the door of the hut, calling out her name. Basa and all her neighbours are being asked to report to the headman's hut. A stranger in a white coat is standing there, a long line of men, women and children stretched out in front of him. He takes out a long needle and jabs it into every extended arm.

Basa doesn't even feel the prick, really. The sting of a red ant is much more potent. And the ant is everywhere. You never knew when it might climb onto your body.

There is an old saying in Gondi, 'The brave one sits on the anthill without crying out.'

Dr Deepak Mehra sits on a stool and certainly feels like he qualifies for a medal of bravery. It has been a long eight-hour journey by road from Raipur to Bastar district. And from there, an open jeep into the jungle, the last half hour on foot. The government had gone mad – they wanted to test random samples in every taluka of every district across the country.

Who would do the job? Young MBBS doctors like him, of course.

A week later, a high-level meeting chaired by Amitabh Kant examines the data from the nationwide effort. And a single figure catches his eye. A tiny backward pocket in Chhattisgarh has zero Covid cases. Was something wrong with the data? A team would have to be dispatched at once, to re-examine the numbers ...

***

Three months later, the *International Journal of Virology* carries a paper written by Dr Mehra, et al: 'The tribals in a remote district of India called Bastar have high natural immunity, thanks to their traditional diet. Alcohol distilled from the mahua plant (*Madhuca longifolia*) is used for treating cold, cough, bronchitis and other respiratory disorders ...'

Researchers also note in the paper that the oft-consumed red ant chutney has strong anti-viral properties.

A Sanjeevani vaccine to combat the novel coronavirus will soon be available ... to all.

Hum Aapke Hain Kaun

THE WEDDING CARD CAME WITH A BOX OF FERRERO Rocher chocolates and the bearer – the father of the groom – insisted on our attendance.

'Na na, I won't listen to any excuses. Haven't we known each other as long as you've lived in this complex? Kitna purana rishta hai hamara.'

To be honest, I didn't feel any great kinship towards him, but ever since we had moved to NCR, we were forced to be more 'social'. In Mumbai, my wife and I attended maybe one wedding a year. In Dillli-Gudgawa, shaadi ka season could mean three shaadis in a day. There was always a mad rush to marry on the 'most auspicious muhurat'.

Most auspicious for the caterer and ghodiwala ... charging mooh-maanga premium.

As always, on the appointed day, the Mrs dressed up in fine clothes and fake jewellery, while I donned my kurta with a Modi jacket. With the help of Google Maps, we reached the venue in our battered, old Maruti Swift. As I handed my keys to the valet, I noticed a number of Mercedes, BMWs and a few Pajeros parked outside.

The baarat was at the gate, but would surely take another hour to make its grand entry. This was indeed the best time to slip in and explore the cornucopia of food. We made a dash for the pani puri stall before it got too crowded. After a world food tour (Mexico, China, Italy and Burma), we returned to India for our just desserts.

My naada is feeling a little tight now, and besides, duty is calling. We stand in the kilometre-long queue with our shagun ka lifafa. When we finally ascend the lavishly decorated stage, we are warmly greeted.

'I am so happy you have come to our function,' said the host, and he genuinely meant it.

We greeted the bride and groom, in matching outfits and *hum-saath-khush-hain* expressions. Followed by the mandatory photo and veedeeo, which will rot in a pen drive for the next twenty years.

Having played our part in another edition of the Big Fat Indian Wedding, we hop off the stage. Before we leave, there is one last ritual – the post-prandial treat.

Let the goras have their Baileys and Peach schnapps. We desis know better. That leaf-encrusted, juice-bombing heaven in two fingers – also known as paan. Nothing tells you the class of a wedding more than the quality of its Banarasi paan. And by that yardstick, this wedding was off the charts.

As we left the pandal, well satisfied, I noticed a helicopter standing near the gate, bedecked with marigolds. Bhai, sab kuch dekha tha. Drones showering rose petals, gold-painted human sculptures, Shahrukh Khan performing ... But this was a first. A ride home which the newly married couple would not forget!

'Achcha tha,' my wife remarked on the way home. 'I could have worn a heavier sari.'

Stuck in bumper-to-bumper shaadi-wala traffic on NH48, I wished I was in that helicopter.

***

Two days later, there was a knock on our door at 6 a.m. It was the milkman, who had been serving us from the day we arrived in the complex.

'Bete ki shaadi toh bahut badhiya kari. Ab toh ghar pe aaraam kar sakte ho,' said my wife.

Ramlal Yadav grinned. He had sold his ancestral lands and become a crorepati. But a man cannot sit at home and do nothing.

Hoon toh main doodhwala; doodh hi toh bechoonga.
Woh bhi paani mila ke.

Child's Play

As a child, Abhaya loved solving puzzles. Every time his father went abroad on a business trip, he had only one demand: 'Baba, just get me a new puzzle ... Big one, bigger than last time.'

Baba was only too happy to oblige. The puzzles only grew more complicated each time Baba travelled. A vast blue sky with 300 almost-identical pieces. A pond with light and dark reflections of trees. The more complex the puzzle, the more Abhaya loved solving it. As his brain made its connections, his nimble fingers put pieces into their rightful places.

Abhaya soon moved on to crosswords and sudoku until, as he grew older, he discovered the joys of algebra. While his friends moaned before their mathematics exam, Abhaya could be found in a zen-like state. What was so difficult about finding the value of x or y? Both sides have to balance, that's all.

'Your boy is very bright,' his Class 9 teacher told his parents. 'He can become a great mathematician!'

Abhaya felt his heart would burst with happiness that day. He dreamt of a day when he would sit in a bare room with white walls, undisturbed by anyone, only in the company of his beloved equations.

But life had other plans.

When Abhaya completed Class 11, the company his father worked for went bust. Newspapers reported about a massive fraud, money siphoned off to tax havens. All employees lost their jobs, but Abhaya's father was implicated in the case. Now, all of the family's time, energy and savings were devoted towards proving Baba's innocence.

Abhaya gave up on his plans to study mathematics in IIT. He enrolled in a local commerce college, which did not require much attendance. He needed a job, any job, to support his family. But who would employ an eighteen-year-old matric pass? As luck would have it, Jamanbhai's stock broking firm was in need of an office boy. And they didn't care much about qualifications for this role.

'Time pe avjo,' was the only condition, and Abhaya had no problem complying with it.

In fact, he was the first to reach the office and the last to leave. The work he did was very basic – fetching tea, making photocopies, attending phone calls. But his thirsty mind drank in everything that was happening around him. Buying long, selling short, margin calls, squaring of positions. After office hours, he would sit and read the printouts and reports lying around. Along with his commerce textbook.

One night, he printed out the balance sheet of M/s Swansong Exports and studied it carefully. Aha, ab samajh mein aa rahi hai baat. Every night, before leaving office, Abhaya photocopied a balance sheet and spent the night poring over it. He circled numbers, made notes. No one could stop him from the pursuit of knowledge.

Goddess Saraswati does not exist only in IIMs; she is everywhere.

One afternoon, Jamanbhai was meeting his brokers. The point of contention was Evergreen Plantations. Maganbhai was of the opinion that the stock was undervalued, but Jamanbhai was hesitant to buy shares. Abhaya had studied this balance sheet just two days ago; the numbers were still fresh. As he served a second round of tea to the room, he said, almost to himself, 'Look at the cash reserves.'

The arrow found its mark. *Something* had been bothering Jamanbhai, but he hadn't been able to pinpoint what it was. He looked at Abhaya in amazement ... Who was this kal ka chhokra?

This diamond in the rough.

***

Abhaya now sits in a bare room with white walls, undisturbed by anyone, only in the company of his beloved equations. The only person allowed to enter is his trusted lieutenant, Jamanbhai.

'Abhaya, CNBC wants to do an interview with you about short-selling in the time of coronavirus.'

Not interested. It was far more important to do the work. To expose the frauds committed by companies, the ones they thought they could get away with. Besides, what would he really say?

'It's a bit like solving a puzzle … it's child's play.'

A Woman of Substance

L̲ALITHA WAS A VIRTUOUS LADY WITH ONLY ONE VICE – A fondness for Kanjeevaram sarees. She had entered her marital home with a small trunk containing two such sarees. They were magnificent, woven from the finest silk, with rich zari borders. And the colours – oh, they were to die for. The customary bridal red, of course. But Lalitha's favourite was the peacock blue.

'Oh, my Chinu,' her husband had said when he saw her draped in it the first time. 'You are my goddess.'

It was the first and last time Ragavan said anything romantic to Lalitha. But it was enough. Over the next forty-six years, he was a responsible husband. On the last day of the month, he came and handed over his entire salary to Lalitha. Unlike those wastrels who blew up their money on alcohol, while the family survived on the cheapest of rice and watery sambhar.

Back then, a clerk's salary was meagre – an honest clerk's even more so. But Lalitha was an efficient money manager. She drove a hard bargain for her extra drumstick, found a way to use every part of every vegetable (including the rind of the watermelon!). But economy must never compromise taste. Even the dourest of relatives agreed that Lalitha's cooking was exceptional.

Her secret lay in the spices. Where other ladies would see the grinding of chillies or turmeric as a chore, Lalitha took pleasure in the task. She could spend hours by the grinding stone, humming bhajans under her breath. When her two sons and daughter returned from school, the house would be filled with inviting aromas and something hot on the stove for them to eat.

'Amma, what have you made today? I can't wait to taste!' the younger boy, Sunder, would exclaim.

The look of joy on their faces always filled Lalitha's heart with love. But, in the blink of an eye, the children grew up. The older son, Shanker, became an engineer with the PWD, while Sunder joined a private company. Her daughter, Sharada, completed her BEd and became a schoolteacher.

With the help of a matchmaker, Shanker married Sujatha. Well, the horoscopes of the bride and groom may have matched, but were in absolute opposition to that of the mother-in-law. Lalitha was gradually sidelined from her own kitchen. She wanted her son to be happy, so she did not make a fuss and quietly bowed out. But things only got worse ...

Sunder got married next and Sangeetha entered the household. She could get along with neither her mother-in-law nor her sister-in-law. So she nagged her husband until he agreed to set up a separate household.

Grandchildren then kept Lalitha occupied for some years, but they too grew up all too soon. The final blow came when Ragavan collapsed one morning after a massive heart attack.

In the weeks and months that followed, Lalitha sank into depression. She sat in her room, staring at the wall. Finally, Sujatha said to her husband, 'Speak to your sister.'

Eighteen years ago, Sharada had stunned her family when she asked for permission to marry a man of her choice. A love marriage and that too outside the community? To a Catholic? Ragavan had sternly told his daughter that if this was what she wanted, he could not stop her. But from then on, she was dead to the rest of the family.

Until now. However, Amma had now become a burden on the brothers who wanted nothing to do with her. Sharada sized up the situation and quietly said to her mother, 'From now on, you will live with me.'

Tears rolled down Lalitha's eyes. She took nothing from that house except the trunk with her three everyday-wear saris and her two precious Kanjeevarams. Sharada's husband, Joseph, lovingly touched Lalitha's feet, while sixteen-year-old

Rahul hugged her tight. Joseph had only one small request of Amma.

'I want to taste the sambhar made by you ... Sharada never stops talking about it!'

Lalitha's eyes lit up. She was finally home.

***

One year later

With 1.2 million subscribers, 'Lalitha's Spice Kitchen' is one of the top ten channels on YouTube. Thanks to her grandson Rahul, who started uploading the videos.

'Lalitha is like my paati, I just love to watch her. Her recipes are so practical and genuine ... All my cooking in the lockdown is only due to her!' gushed Gayathri, a Tamil film actress on Twitter. Thus increasing page views by ten times.

Soon, very soon, Lalitha will have as many Kanjeevarams as her heart desires.

State of Mind

Like every other small businessman in the country, Puneet was hit by Hurricane Covid. It swept away his sales, destroyed his supply chain and wiped out his cash flow. He was now hanging from a frayed rope called hope on the edge of a cliff called bankruptcy. As the world was baking banana bread, Puneet's whole life seemed like a giant rotten banana.

He sat with his head in his hands, thinking things couldn't possibly get worse.

But they did. The live-in maid, who held the Mehra house aloft, disappeared a day after lockdown was announced. She did not want to risk catching the 'ameeron ki bimaari' from her employer, who travelled abroad frequently. So, along with the collapse of his business, Puneet now had to become Sanjeev Kapoor in the kitchen and Kantabai at the sink.

His china-doll wife, Gitika, didn't even know how to turn on the stove, let alone boil an egg. The only child of a rich industrialist father, she was spoilt silly. For Daddy, the marriage was a strategic gambit. A nice Khatri boy with an IIM degree was just what his legacy business needed. But that's not quite how it unfolded.

One look at sasurji's hawaai chappal factory in Meerut and Puneet knew he could never work there. Or live in that city. And a wise decision it was. Sasurji was not a man who knew how to delegate. Instinctively, Puneet hung on to his job with McQuigley and Company, moving from London to New York to Johannesburg.

Gitika excelled as a McQuigley wife. With the aid of super-expensive nannies and maids on every continent. For Puneet, it was a small price to pay. Over the years, sasurji had accepted the situation, but remained bitter about it. On one of their annual trips to India, after a peg of Blue Label Johnny Walker, he surveyed his indentured son-in-law and remarked, 'Kitna bhi tum salary le lo, apne kaam ka mazaa kuch aur hai.'

The arrow hit its mark. Perhaps because despite all the globetrotting and the perks of his job, Puneet was feeling an emptiness inside. One week later, he was on a flight to Mumbai and that was when he saw someone with a book called *Stay Hungry Stay Foolish*. Intrigued, he bought it from the airport bookstore and began reading it. By the time he reached Trident Hotel Nariman Point, he'd finished two chapters.

Puneet sat up all night, devouring the book. In the morning, he switched on his laptop and sent his boss a resignation letter. One month later, he was in Mumbai, registering his company, hiring his first employee, making his business plan. Tough stuff, but if you could get your kid admission in Royal Scottish School, anything was possible.

Although Gitika was petulant at first about the move, she quickly adjusted. The kitty party and hot mom circuit was much more advanced in India. And the fashion was more fun. Using Porter's Framework and McQuigley's strategy, Puneet managed to get his business to a respectable Rs 10-crore turnover. But there, it was stuck.

He attended conferences, watched TED talks, enrolled for online courses. Everyone said just one thing: 'Think out of the box'. But Puneet only felt more boxed in. Maybe he was just a good manager; not a visionary. One who could deal with the present, but not imagine the future.

One evening, while he was pondering on this very question, he slipped into a trance.

It was all so clear suddenly – the path the company should take, the hard decisions required.

Every day, Puneet worked to make things happen. Bit by bit by bit. At night, he followed a fixed routine, which became the problem-solving part of his day. At the Economic Times Start-up Awards 2023, Puneet Mehra was celebrated as one of the ten entrepreneurs who emerged from Covid-19 as winners.

On stage, he said, 'I was hungry, I was foolish, and I married the right woman.'

***

That evening, Puneet returned home, went straight into the kitchen. This was his favourite part of the day – when he got all his best ideas.

'If only the *ET* guys knew my little secret …' he chuckled.

Meditation takes on many different forms. Some need a Himalayan cave, some need a sink full of dirty dishes.

Chal Meri Dhanno

∞

Babita woke up at first light and stretched out her tiny frame. Despite eight hours of deep sleep, every muscle and every joint in her body was sore. She went to the washroom and splashed water on her face. She had been wearing the same set of clothes for six days now. But it didn't matter – for the worst was behind her.

'Le, kha le ek alu ka paratha,' said the petrol pump wale bhaiyya. 'Tujhe taakat ki zaroorat hai.'

105 km to Darbhanga, but 995 km from Gurgaon. That's how far she had come.

As Babita sipped sweet, milky tea, she said a prayer to Hanumanji, who had given her the strength to take on this impossible task. When she first told her mother the audacious plan, Munni Devi was shocked. 'Arey, pagli, yeh toh na ho payega.' But there was no alternative.

No bus, no train. People were telling her to wait a while longer. Magar kab tak? The landlord was threatening to throw them – and their meagre belongings – out on the road. 'Na re, better to leave before that,' Babita had told her mother. 'You don't worry, I will figure out something.' For in these four months, the fifteen-year-old had learnt to be resourceful.

When she first came to Gurgaon from her village, Babita was overwhelmed. Badi badi building, alag tarah ke log. She had come to help Baba, after his horrible accident. The owner of the auto rickshaw refused to contribute a single rupee towards his treatment. So Amma took a loan for Rs 15,000 from her SHG group.

'Dhyaan se kharach karna,' she had told Babita. Though it need not have been said at all.

Babita quickly realized that the big city was expensive. Medicines, food, rent – they all swallowed up money. So in the afternoons, Babita started working as a maid in a nearby high-rise building. After all, she was an expert in ghar ka kaam. But on 25 March, everything changed. Her employer called her and said, 'Kal se mat aana.'

Why? 'Ek nayi bimaari phail rahi hai,' said the jeep with a loudspeaker. As if that was something to be afraid of, Babita thought. In the village, one or the other bimaari was always spreading. Anyway, the long and short of it was that she was stuck in Gurgaon. Had Baba been well, they could have started walking home, like everyone else. Alas …

When Munni Devi got an SMS saying she had got Rs 500 credit in her Jan Dhan account, Babita knew what she had to do. Gathering the last bit of her savings, she made the purchase from a neighbour. Baba was aghast when he was told what to do. Log mujh par hasenge, was his worry. Besides, how would this frail little girl manage this superhuman feat?

But she had.

'Chal, meri Dhanno!' Babita said under her breath. Don't let me down today.

With only her dupatta to shield her face from the sun, Babita gathered her strength for the last leg of the journey. That day, she dreamt of her future. She dreamt of going back to school. Maybe even becoming a teacher. And, one day in the distant future, Babita imagined herself sitting in an aeroplane. Ab kab aur kaise hoga, yeh to pata nahin …

When they finally reached Chamoli at 9 p.m., the sarpanch (wearing a mask) personally welcomed father and daughter. For news had spread about Babita Kumari cycling 1,100 km from Gurgaon to Bihar, with her father riding pillion. A father who had tears in his eyes. For he remembered that long-ago day when he cursed himself for being the unlucky man with three daughters and no son.

'You are my Shravan Kumar,' he said to Babita in the quarantine centre. The little girl's heart swelled with pride. What more could she ask for?

***

A week later, Babita Kumari received a call from the president of the Cycling Federation of India. What stamina, what determination!

'Aapko hum national team mein shaamil karna chahte hain … Uske liye Dilli mein trial hoga.'

They had even promised to send an air ticket! But, deep inside, Babita knew, what she really wanted to do.

'Chal, meri Dhanno! Le chal mujhe school.'

Taking a Chance

~∂~

TATHAGATA CHATTERJEE LED A ROUTINE AND PREDICTABLE life – and that's the way he liked it. He had been a studious schoolboy, sincere college student and, now, he was a conscientious professor of chemistry at Sarat Bose College of Arts and Science in Kolkata. It was a good job, with fixed hours and a fixed salary. What more could a Bangla bandhu ask for?

'I am not in this rat race, you know,' he would tell Ashok, his childhood friend, who was a successful Marwari businessman.

What did these Marwaris know anyway? They'd never had the pleasure of eating chingri malai curry or kosha mangsho. Nor would they spend an afternoon playing chess or discussing the macropraxis of alienation at the College Street Coffee House. No, baba, those chaps were too busy making money. And more money. And even more money.

One evening, as was his habit, Tathagata babu stopped by the local barber shop, in need of a haircut. But there was a long line of people awaiting their turn. It was especially urgent to get it done, in view of the NAAC inspection of the college the next morning. So he took the quick decision of entering the fancy 'Air-Cool Men's Saloon' next door.

As the name suggested, it was air-conditioned. Which was welcome relief from Kolkata's heat. A smart young man in a uniform beckoned him onto a padded chair and asked what kind of cut sir would like. Tathagata was secretly thrilled at this deferential treatment. As for what cut, well, he had no clue, but pointed to the cover of the magazine lying on the table in front of him.

'Bhalo, sir, bhalo choice,' said the young man and began snipping away.

Enveloped in the sweet scent of fancy hair oils and serums, sipping a cup of herbal tea, Tathagata slipped away into the land of dreams. Didn't he deserve to pamper himself once in a while?

In this altered state of consciousness, the loud voice of a man sitting next to him pierced his very soul.

'Buy Naveen Castings; buy it, I tell you,' said the voice. '100 per cent returns assured in six months.'

Tathagata was shocked. When fixed deposits yielded 7.2 per cent (compound interest), what was this giving 100 per cent returns? He pretended to watch himself in the mirror, but his ears strained to follow Mr 100 Per Cent. In the process, he ended up having a head massage (heavenly), a shave and a trim (so luxurious). When the helpful young man suggested a manicure, Tathagata finally called it a day.

And just as well, because, when he got the bill at the counter, Tathagata almost fainted. The two hours he had spent at the salon cost him Rs 600 (plus GST). Why, this was highway robbery! But what could he do now – create a fuss? He was in a foul mood at home that night and bitterly criticized his wife's cooking.

The next day, he met Ashok and asked him about Naveen Castings. It was a large company, listed on the stock exchange. What about it?

'Can you buy 100 shares for me?' asked Tathagata.

Ashok was surprised. His friend had never ever shown an interest in making money. But it was a simple enough request. Soon, at the end of six months, the Rs 25,000 Tathagata had spent were indeed Rs 50,000. And that is how he became a regular customer of Air-Cool Men's Saloon – including a manicure and pedicure – on Thursday evenings.

Ready and waiting for the next big tip to fall into his wax-cleaned ears.

***

April 2020

Tathagata Chatterjee now sits still as his wife, Patralekha, holds forth on his reckless behaviour. Useless fellow threw Rs 25,000 in the gutter …

'Then you go to that salon also and waste more money!' she shrieked.

Good luck, Mr Chatterjee. You've taken a haircut on your foolish investment; now prepare yourself for the real thing. For hell hath no fury like a woman with scissors in her hand.

Real Medicine

॰֍॰

It was 3 p.m. when Dr Tanu finally finished with her last patient. She felt tired, but was satisfied with the day's work. For a moment, Tanu stared outside her window, drinking in the fiery-red leaves of the gulmohar tree. The afternoon was extremely hot, but within the mud-brick walls of Jeevan Clinic, a fan was sufficient.

'Didi, kya hai … Aapko khane ki bhi fursat nahin. Lo, ab to jeem lo.'

Savitabai put down a thali with chane ki dal lauki, garam-garam rotis and namkeen sev on Tanu's desk. The young doctor gave her a grateful smile. In the eighteen months that she had spent in rural Madhya Pradesh, working at a primary health centre, Savitabai had been a lifeline. Her cheerful personality and native intelligence made her a valuable assistant to the doctor. In every possible sense.

Mumbai now seemed a lifetime away. Those MBBS days when life was all about lectures, hospital rounds, gappa sessions in the canteen, talks about the future – who was planning to go abroad, who could pay Rs 2 crore for a post-grad seat in surgery ... It was all about money, how to earn it and how to spend it. None of this appealed to Tanu.

One evening, she came across an article on the 'New India' website about Doctor Saathi. They were seeking young medicos who were willing to work in the villages for two years.

A month later, Dr Tanu was on a train to Gwalior, en route to village Chhapra, tehsil Bhitarwar. A community which had been identified as one of the most backward in the state.

'Tum dactarni ho?' asked the sarpanch, shaking his head. Ek toh ladki bheji, aur wo bhi itni chhoti si.

Reluctantly, he took her to the primary health centre. A dilapidated structure with dingy living quarters attached. That afternoon, Dr Tanu put her head in her hands and cried tears of despair. What had she got herself into? When, all of a sudden, she felt a gentle hand on her shoulder. A stout, middle-aged lady was standing there, broom in hand.

Wordlessly, she swept and swabbed the floor, opened all the windows and drew a rangoli outside the door. Suddenly, the place did not look so drab any more. Besides, there was so much work to do ...

Over the next fortnight, Tanu forgot that she was a doctor. She accompanied Savitabai, an anganwadi worker, and learnt what it was really like to live here. Simple things that she had taken for granted in Mumbai were hard to find here. Clean water, electricity, a school with teachers ... Although Maggi and Coca-Cola were everywhere.

Everyone was curious about the young dactarni. Was she married? How come she lived alone so far from home? Why didn't she sport a bindi? Wo toh sabhi pehente hain ...

'Yeh lo, didi,' said one newly married girl, sticking a small red dot on her forehead.

Well, if that's what it took to get accepted ... theek hai. It took some months for Tanu to realize one simple truth. Diarrhoea, anaemia, iodine deficiency ... These were preventable. The young doctor arranged for iron tablets, vitamins and iodine patches to be sent. And got them distributed among all the pregnant women in the village.

But a month later, Savitabai came with disturbing news. A lot of women did not take the pills regularly. Some even believed that bachche ka rang kaala ho jayega. Dr Tanu did not know whether to laugh or cry ... Nothing taught in medical school had prepared her for this moment. She looked at herself in the bathroom mirror – a young woman with a dusty face, tired eyes and a crooked bindi.

Eureka!

***

Medical News Today: 'A young doctor in rural Madhya Pradesh has come up with a unique way of reducing iodine deficiency among women. With the help of a local manufacturer, Dr Tanushree Kulkarni has created an iodine patch which can be worn in the form of a bindi …'

Women were thrilled to receive a free supply of these bindis … And would wear them without fuss. When Dr Tanu looks at herself in the mirror, she sees a doctor who has left her textbook behind.

Because real medicine is not about the disease, but lies in understanding the patient.

Faking It

🌀

Wu Jiabao leaned back in his leather armchair and put his feet up on the mahogany desk. From the corner of his eye, he glanced at the feed of the CCTV camera streaming continuously on his iMac. From his super-chilled air-conditioned office, he could see the factory floor from twelve different angles.

'Keep one eye open even while you sleep,' was what his grandmother used to say.

And one could never be vigilant enough. The workers in his factory were from the hinterland, which was very different from the glass and steel of Shanghai. These men and women were willing to do anything for a better life. Living far from home and family, in tiny, cramped houses – they were happy to simply have this job.

His Italian buyer was amazed – and a little resentful – of how hard his people were willing to work. Twelve-hour shifts were normal, but they could easily stretch to fourteen or even sixteen. The trick he had learnt early on was to keep them well-fed. A dozen rice cookers and generous portions kept stomachs full. And ensured that the rumble of discontent was kept at bay.

It wasn't the workers, but that snoopy journalist who created all the problems. She came to the factory pretending to be a prospective buyer. Three weeks later, she wrote that horrible article titled 'Your Lucci bag was made in a sweatshop'. What was her problem, exactly? The work was top-class and every worker was here out of their free will.

'These Westerners are so soft and namby-pamby,' he often said to his wife, Shan Shan.

Their ancestors had the hunger to sail to distant lands, conquer the native people, plunder their resources and make themselves rich. But that was a couple of hundred years ago. The new generation had no interest in working hard. After all, they had the legacy of the past to fall back on. Naturally, the Chinese took advantage of that.

Wu himself was a perfect example of how far industry and hard work could get you in life. He had travelled far from his village to make his fortune. He worked his way up from the very bottom of the ladder to the very top. Had he done it all ethically? Maybe not. One can only do charity when there is money in the pocket.

In less than two decades, Wu was running a flourishing business making fake designer handbags. All was going well until, one day, he got a surprise visit from Mr Vespuccio Lucci himself. It was the one time Wu was struck dumb. The ground fell away from under his feet as he imagined various worst-case scenarios.

'Young man,' said the seventy-seven-year-old Italian. 'If you really want to make high-quality designer handbags, do it for me.'

So it was a win-win for both. Yes, there was the occasional blip like that article. But most journalists were happy enough to receive a free Lucci bag on Christmas and look the other way. Of course, many a time, Wu did wonder what people saw in these bags. They were, after all, a few nice pieces of leather. Stitched by hand.

The only thing that made the bag worth $20,000 was the label that was stuck on it. A piece of metal to which society attached so much significance.

With China being one of the most lucrative markets for luxury goods. A country whose land was never colonized by the West, but whose mind was now colonized by their brands. How fake and pointless it all was.

***

Wu Jiabao left the factory in his BMW and sped home, through the Tuscan countryside. Two decades after being smuggled to Italy, he still could not get enough of the scenery.

'To sell our goods, we must understand the psyche of the customer,' Mr Lucci always said.

Nobody cares that the bags are sewn by Chinese hands. As long as they are 'Made in Italy'.

A Matter of Pride

The minutes just before a race is about to begin are the longest. Everything the athlete could possibly do has been done. Now, it's all in the hands of destiny.

This was the most important race of Jerome's life. He had spent seven years training for just this moment. Waking up each morning at 5 a.m., reporting for practice at 5.30 a.m. Warm-ups and stretching, followed by one mile ins and outs. Walk, sprint, walk, sprint, walk. Back to the hostel for a protein-rich breakfast, which never failed to gladden his heart.

The very first day, when Jerome saw twelve boiled eggs on his plate, tears pricked his eyes. Never had he seen such abundance. Why, his entire family could have eaten this and still had leftovers!

'Eat up, my boy,' said Coach Nipon, as if he could read the young lad's mind. 'You need it.'

He had seen many promising boys, just like Jerome. Picked them up from villages where they played football in the mud. Or spotted them at the races held during the harvest festival. Yet, never had he seen a talent like Jerome. The boy moved with the speed of a gazelle and the fierceness of a cheetah. He was lithe and supple; however what really stood out was his attitude.

A race, after all, is run with the body but won with the mind.

The whistle sounded for the sprinters to take their places on the starting block. Jerome stretched his sinewy body one last time and strode forth with confidence. As he took his position, a bead of sweat glistened on his forehead. To his left, was the triple world record–holder, Angus Maxwell. To his right was Olympic legend Michael Mahala.

As expected, all eight athletes in the 100-metres dash finals at the 2021 Tokyo Olympics were Black. But some were 'more equal' than others.

The American had been groomed from an early age, using the latest technology. His every stride recorded, analysed, strategized, optimized. To make sure he peaked at 'just the right time'. The Jamaican had the benefit of training at the Usain Bolt Academy, with the latest facilities and a role model who believed in the potential of each boy.

As for Jerome, he came from a country which rarely made its presence felt at the Olympics. The national sporting federation was mired in politics, more interested in making money off athletes' kits than their performance. It was only when he won his first international race that they sat up and took notice of his talent. Jerome became a hot Olympic prospect, which came with its own set of problems.

'Run; run like the wind!' were his father's final words to Jerome, as he boarded the plane to Tokyo.

As the whistle blew, the weight of the country's expectations slipped off his young shoulders. Jerome felt light; he felt free. The gun went off.

'Maxwell has gotten a good enough start; Mahala was a bit slow to begin. He's got some work to do. Jerome coming in Maxwell ... In front, Jerome stretching out now. *He's coming after him! He's done it, my god!* In 9.63 seconds! A new Olympic record!'

Jerome was still running. He was running from his past. He was running for his future.

He was running for every poor village boy who did not have shoes.

***

As 'Jana Gana Mana' was played, Olympic gold medallist Jerome Siddi burst into tears. And 1.3 billion Indians cried tears of joy with him.

The Prime Minister tweeted: 'A nation salutes its son for bringing glory with an Olympic gold medal. Jerome Siddi's ancestors came to India from Africa centuries ago and made India their home. This is the unity in diversity of the great civilization called India.'

Jaya he, jaya he, jaya he,
Jaya jaya jaya jaya he.

Main Shayar toh Nahin

Waise to mehfil kisi hall mein jamti hai,
Is waqt to ghar ka hall hi mehfil hai.
Toh aaiye, haath mein jaam lijiye,
Apni health ko salaam kijiye.
Aap ke naak, kaan, haath salaamat hain,
Aapki samajhdaari hi amaanat hai.
Bank mein chand rupaye mehfooz hain,
Ghar mein atta–dal aur juice hain.
Kya pata tha duniya itni badal jayegi,
March ka haseen mahina yeh rang layegi.
Yeh ajeeb dastaan kab tak chalegi,
Coronavirus kis vaccine se maregi.

Aur uske baad duniya kaisi dikhegi,
Kya Chanel ki bag phir bhi bikegi.
Faltu cheezon par kharche ki aadat,
Khuda se badhkar paise ki ibaadat.
Five-star ke khaane ka shaukeen,
Credit card se sab kuch mumkeen.
Aur agar paise bachane ki gustaakhi ki hai,
Usey bank mein rakhna kaafi nahi hai.
Experts TV par naseehat dete hain,
Unki baat hum seriously lete hain.
Magar kya unko kuch aata hai?
Kyunki jitna profit utna ghaata hai.
Ek janaab Franklin Templeton ke naam se,
Bechaare corona mein gaye wo kaam se,
Lekin shikaar hue woh haalat se,
Ya ek virus se badi baat se?
Laalach kehte hain buri bala hai,
Lekin MBAs ke liye woh bhi kala hai.
Jawaan ko jhurriyon ki cream bech do,
Mehnat ki kamaai ko jad se khench do.
Naye naye tarah ke ishtihaar nikaal do,
Khwaabon ki duniya mein janta ko daal do.
Har ghar mein ho Maggi aur Coke,
Na ho khidki, na ho shauch,
Mumbai ki sattar feesadi aabaadi,
Corona ne kari unki barbaadi.
Jhuggi ke woh mehnati insaan,
Jinka aaj chhin gaya imaan.

Do waqt ki roti unhe naseeb nahin,
Kai ke to ghar bhi kareeb nahin.
Phanse hue hain anjaan sheher main,
Na bus na train is pahar mein.
Duniya ka har desh soch raha hai,
Capitalism gala daboch raha hai.
Vaccine agar ban bhi jaaegi,
Kya sab ke hisse mein aaegi?
Ya phir hamesha ki tarah kuch log,
Beshumaar profit ka karenge bhog.
Jaise ki China ke kaarkhaane,
Lagein hue hain mask banane.

Pehle to khaya chimgadad ka bachcha,
Ketchup ke saath ya yun hi kachcha.
Ab toh aap samajh gaye honge,
Lucknow se hain toh ro pade honge.
Haan main asli shayar toh nahin,
Magar jab zindagi hi nakli si ho gayi,
Toh shayar kya nacheez hai.
Ab tanhaee mein asliyat nazar aa rahi hai,
Shayad bhaag daud ki duniya mein,
Lautne ki chahat hi na ho.

Think Pink

When the pink slip came via email, Swati was actually relieved. Everyone knew the company that she worked for was screwed by Covid. With Work from Home suddenly becoming *the* thing, who the hell was going to buy formal wear and office clothes? It seemed ages ago when one actually ironed clothes … Or even wore a bra.

'So what's the plan, now, behna?' asked her flatmates, Pragati and Niyati. There was no plan.

For the first week, Swati just slept, binged Netflix and slept some more. After completing all the episodes of *Miss Fisher's Murder Mysteries*, both seasons of *Four More Shots Please* and *Panchayat*, she'd finally had enough. Or, well, the broadband quota for the month was exhausted and her flatmates were really, really mad.

So, Swati turned her attention to the kitchen. Someone was posting all kinds of yummy-looking cupcakes and breads on the NIFT WhatsApp group. Chalo, try karte hain. After a few trial-and-error cakes (which were either too hard or completely flat), a perfect vanilla sponge was finally produced. With chocolate frosting. All was forgiven by the flatmates.

Now this hobby may have carried Swati through the lockdown, except that she ran out of baking powder. And baking soda and yeast. What's more, all these items were out of stock on Big Basket, Nature's Basket and even Amazon! Pragati and Niyati were kind of relieved when they heard that Swati wouldn't be able to bake any more. What with no exercise and too many cravings ... Achha hi hua.

'Why don't you start something of your own,' they suggested. And Swati did have an idea ...

When she shared it, her flatmates lit up. 'Fantastic, we would definitely buy this product!' they exclaimed. But Swati had no clue how to go about it. Until Niyati, an industrial engineer, came up with the plan. Using her knowledge of CAD/CAM, she could surely design a prototype. Which they could get 3D printed ...

The trouble was getting specifications to design the damn thing. That was where Pragati stepped in with a solution. 'We collect data online – from folks we know – and I can then use it to design an algorithm. What is an underworked computer engineer for, anyway?'

Soon, it all came together, like it was destiny. Though it took way longer than they had thought.

But when the prototype finally arrived, there was a collective whoop of joy. This was exactly what the world needed, post lockdown. Now all they needed was money. To go into production. Pragati asked her IIT classmate – who was now an ISB graduate – for advice. After all, Dipti worked for a well-known venture capital firm.

'Sounds interesting, but hardly the kind of idea that gets funded,' was her truthful response. 'But, hey, I'd like to buy one,' Dipti added. 'Why don't you start a crowdfunding campaign?'

That evening, the three musketeers – as they now called themselves – listed the product on Kickstarter. They described it as a revolutionary offering, which would change everyday lives. Help its users defy limitations, defy norms. Even defy gravity.

All they needed was Rs 6 lakh to manufacture the first lot. Would you like to be one of our first customers?

Twenty-four hours later, they had raised Rs 5 lakh. By the next day, it was Rs 8 lakh. Whoopeeee, they were in business!

Who knew that a team of three women in lockdown could put their heads together and create something that made a real and tangible difference?

Who knows what else is possible …?

***

Reported by ET Now, six months later: 'A startup led by three women has just received funding from Pixel Partners of an undisclosed amount. Their product "Perfecto"™, the bra that fits just right, has been receiving rave reviews online.

'"There has been little or no innovation in this industry for the last 100 years," said Latha Shastri, senior partner at Pixel and an early adopter.

'The company's motto: "Designed by humans with boobs for humans with boobs."

'May they continue to defy gravity and society for years to come.'

Path of Destiny

༄

Pandit Umashankar Tripathi was a taskmaster. But even he could find no fault with the boy's recitation. Sanskrit shlokas were rolling off his tongue like the mighty Ganges flowing through Haridwar. Panditji was exhilarated. There were many students in the gurukul, but none as bright, as sincere or as intense as Mani.

'Finally, I have found the one who will carry forth my legacy,' he thought.

Panditji was one of the few living repositories of ancient esoteric knowledge, handed down from guru to shishya, generation after generation. He traced his own lineage back to the Saptarishis, the seven mind-born sons of Brahma. It is believed that they possessed Divya Shakti – extraordinary powers – which was lost to the world over the centuries.

This precious vidya was granted only to the deserving soul, whose purity was unblemished. For one whose *citta* – or mental body – was contaminated with greed and lust, would only abuse and misuse this knowledge. Instead of transmuting the energies and achieving a higher level of consciousness.

During the day, Panditji held discourses on the atman, brahman and the philosophy of Advaita (non-duality) for all his shishyas. But late in the night, when all were asleep, Mani received Brahmvidya from his Guru. Like a USB drive downloading data from a PC, connected to the mainframe. Simply sitting across from one another. No words were exchanged.

When Mani was eleven years old, Panditji called him and said, 'My son, I have made a difficult decision. You must leave the ashram.'

Mani was stunned. He could not understand where he had failed his guru; what had gone wrong? But he accepted the diktat without questioning it – Panditji could not be wrong.

Mani returned to his parents' home, enrolled in a school and began leading a regular life. It wasn't easy, initially, but he was extremely bright. And there was something about him that made the bullies stay away. The peculiar little boy found solace in the world of science. He became a permanent fixture in the school library, a role model often held up by his teachers.

At Presidency College, where he enrolled for a BSc in physics, Mani came to be known as 'Junior Einstein' – thanks to his wild hairstyle and brilliance in the subject. No one was surprised when Mani secured a full scholarship for an MS at the Max Planck Institute in Germany. This was followed by a PhD and then a fellowship at CERN in Geneva.

In 2012, CERN made a startling announcement: 'Continuous experiments conducted with the Large Hadron Collider confirm the existence of the Higgs-Boson. An elementary particle produced by the excitation of the Higgs field.' Since no journalist could quite understand that, they simply called it the 'god particle'.

Mani, who was part of the team at CERN, had a sudden flashback. The guru was speaking to him.

'Brahman is not a He or a She – it is a field; it is the basis of everything. And everything is just its own reflection. It is neither a thing nor is it nothing.'

Quantum physics, his life's passion, was just a reflection of his study of Vedanta. Two sides of the same coin.

He was indeed the Chosen One.

***

Thirty-one years later

At a glittering ceremony in the city of Stockholm, Dr Mani received the Nobel Prize for Physics. The citation read as follows:

'For transforming physics by identifying and quantifying, the basic building block of matter – CUs, or units of Consciousness. The interaction of CUs with thought waves creates our reality – and multiple realities – simultaneously, inter-dimensionally. Thus, completing the elusive String Theory.'

The mission that destiny had ordained was complete. Science and spirituality would never have to be at war again.

Memories of Midnight

❦

Ruchika adjusted the camera until she got her frame. The old lady was sitting on a charpoy, the light falling on her wrinkled face. Ruchika prayed that the interview would go well, for it was the last one she needed to complete her PhD and this ambitious project. She nodded at Beeji's daughter-in-law sitting nearby and pressed 'start' on the camcorder.

'Beeji, *twada* interview *lain waaste kudi aayi si*,' said the younger woman to her mother-in-law. 'Do you remember anything … from the time of Partition?'

Beeji looked bemused. What kind of question was that? Who could ever forget? But, like so many others of her generation, she had spent a lifetime trying to do just that. Yet, today, sitting in her aangan, in front of this expectant young woman, something stirred inside Beeji. It was time to tell her story ... who knew how much longer she had?

The old lady was lost in thought for several minutes. Ruchika sat still; she said nothing. For an interview must be allowed to unfold. Finally, Beeji found her voice.

'What should I say?

'Well, this is my story. But it's not mine alone; there were hundreds and thousands like me. I was one of the lucky ones. I survived.

'I was sixteen years old in the year 1947. We lived in Surjanwala, a village 80 km from Lahore. It was the month of September, when the trouble began. We heard that mobs were roaming around the countryside, armed with sticks and spears. Murdering the men and abducting the women. Young girls of my age were jumping into the well, to save their izzat.

'"We must leave for India," said bauji, with tears in his eyes. There was no alternative. We left with just the clothes on our back, and made it to the station in the dead of the night.

'My chacha lived in the adjacent house. He was a rich man – a tax collector – and he had a lot of jewellery and cash in the locker. The last I remember of him, he was busy packing it all into suitcases. We waited and waited, but they never arrived. We later heard that they got caught on the way. Jaan se bhi gaye, maal se bhi.

'Our coach was packed with men, women and children. We sat there for hours – hungry and thirsty, desperate for the train to start moving. And finally it did ... But when we reached Lahore, out of nowhere, a mob appeared. They began jumping onto the footboard, hanging onto the windows. We saw the madness in their eyes and knew what was to come.

'In that moment, I thought, everything is over. Magar Waheguru ki kripa, Waheguru ki fateh. We were saved. All of a sudden, the train picked up speed. Those mad young men loosened their grip and disappeared from sight. The train did not make any stops till we reached Amritsar. Bas ... that's the how we came to India and started a new life.'

'Sattar saal ho gaye si,' she said wistfully and a tear rolled down her cheek. Ruchika clasped Beeji's frail hands in her own and looked into the old woman's eyes with sincere gratitude. With this, she would finally be able to complete her project – a documentary on the survivors of the Partition. Of whom so few were still alive, and even fewer had their memory intact.

Beeji looked into the eyes of this young woman she had met for the very first time and felt an ajeeb sa apnapan. She untied the knot in the corner of her dupatta and extracted a small object. It was a single coin, her only nishaani from an era bygone. It had travelled with her in a train from Pakistan and never left her side since.

'Le, puttar,' she said, putting her hand on Ruchika's head. 'Tu bada nek kaam kar rahi hai.'

After many, many, many years, that night, Beeji slept like a baby.

***

Six months later
Ruchika Mehra received the Golden Peacock at the Sarajevo International Film Festival for her documentary, *Memories of Midnight*. While accepting the award, she said, 'I am here today only because of an eighty-six-year-old survivor of the Partition, who showered her blessings on me.'

The shagun she had received from Beeji was, in fact, a 1939 King George silver rupee, lapped up for Rs 5 lakh by a coin collector. Exactly the sum needed to ensure the film had an international release.

Mistress of Spices

❦

She was a delicate English rose; he was the hardy Indian money plant. Well, as they say, opposites attract, so little wonder that Hitesh swooned the first time Helen walked past him in the corridors of Sussex Business School. She smelt of lavender and fresh rain, while he carried the faint smell of curry. Thanks to the ever-present theplas in his bag.

'What's that?' Helen asked, when she spied him munching on them in the cafeteria.

She had only ever eaten naan breads in an Indian restaurant. With chicken tikka masala. Hitesh was only too happy to share the 'tayplas' purchased weekly from Ramnik

Indian Store. To be eaten only with Ba's chhundo. Sweet pickle made from mango, he explained. One bite and Helen thought she had tasted heaven.

This was why Christopher Columbus set sail to India, why Vasco de Gama travelled around the Cape of Good Hope. Why ships full of the Dutch and the British followed. Bloody spices! And 500 years later, the English were still eating bland and lifeless food. They hadn't progressed beyond black pepper and paprika. Maybe a dash of cinnamon.

There are many ways to patao a girl – chocolates, flowers, maybe an Amazon gift card. Hitesh's wily Gujarati brain went a step further. He presented a stainless-steel masala box to Helen. The standard one found in every Indian household, with rai, jeera, dhaniya powder, mirchi and haldi.

This was the perfect introduction to Indian cooking.

'Oh, Hitesh,' said Helen. 'You are so sweet and practical.'

Indeed, Hitesh was unlike any of the boys Helen had dated. He was shy, decent and helpful. When Helen's mother heard about him, she quickly pronounced that he was marriage material. Young Englishmen were louts, with no character, no commitment. 'In this global world, does the colour of one's skin really matter? Go for it, my girl!' she said.

It was one thing to like someone (that could not be helped!), but quite another to go beyond that. Left to himself, Hitesh would never have made any kind of move. Fair Helen understood this and took matters into her own hands. The two quickly became inseparable, without actually becoming a couple. And finally, she invited Hitesh for a weekend at her parent's country mansion.

A sprawling estate with gardens, fountains and elaborate bannisters supporting the many staircases. Hitesh was impressed, but not overawed. Every student at Sussex Business School's family business programme was the offspring of a rich businessman. Godhoomal and Sons was a 115-year-old business with a commanding market share in its category.

Every month, one of his uncles or cousins boarded a plane to Kazakhstan to buy the best possible raw materials, striking a tough bargain with the sellers. It was a near monopoly and a lucrative one at that. Hitesh could talk for hours about the many dimensions of the Ferula extract, its processing and quality control. But he was a guest, so out of politeness, he asked Helen's father, 'Sir, what business is your family in?'

'Perfume, my boy! Rose, lavender, jasmine … Anything with fragrance!'

No wonder Helen always smelt so divine. With a sinking feeling, Hitesh knew there was no future for the two of them. They were Romeo and Juliet, Heer–Ranjha, Shirin–Farhad. Doomed forever.

Unless Helen was brave enough and strong enough to pass the Ultimate Test.

***

She had been warned about the sights and smells of India. But nothing prepared Helen for what hit her when she entered the factory of Godhoomal & Sons. She promptly fainted.

'Oh, my love,' she said, fluttering open her eyelids at last. 'We do belong to two different worlds. But we will make it work!'

They call it 'devil's dung' and it's one of the spices Vasco da Gama never carried back home. Hing, to you and me, jiska swaad gorey kabhi samajh nahin payenge.

Let's hope love conquers all!

Stand by Me

※

The stench of hot tar suffocated Leela as she lay face down on the sidewalk. Her hands were cuffed behind her back. 'Stay still,' said a voice within. 'Be calm. Do *not* think of the worst.'

But how? The murder of George Floyd had shaken all of America and its belief in fairness and justice. And at this moment, she was living proof of it.

'I am with the press,' she spluttered, wishing she could reach for the identity card in her back pocket.

A moment earlier, she had been following a crowd of protestors as they raised their fists and slogans against the injustice. 'Black lives matter,' they chanted. Leela noted the smattering of white faces in the crowd. Like vanilla sprinkles on a chocolate cake. No desis, no sir. We were all too busy keeping out of 'other people's business'. Besides, we were brown-skinned too ...

But that was *different* from being Black. Leela had argued this, many a time, with her mom and dad. 'India is the most racist country of all,' she said. 'Look how much importance we give to fair skin. Fairness creams. Fair brides. In a country which gets so much sun, all people do was to hide from it. And now, they have to consume vitamin D tablets!'

Her mom just shook her head – this was a difficult child. Not like her elder daughter, Geeta, who was so sensible. A normal high-IQ desi, who went to medical school and was now completing her residency. Someone they could proudly talk about at the potluck dinners they went to, where food was secondary to discussing their children and showing off their achievements.

'Mom, Dad, I want to switch my major,' Leela had announced during her junior year at UC Berkeley.

Yes, all her life she'd dreamt of becoming an engineer, but college had changed her. All the 'side stuff' she had dabbled in – anthropology, sociology, gender studies – suddenly seemed so much more fascinating. A stint at the campus newspaper convinced Leela that her calling lay in words and not algorithms.

Of course, no one at home could understand what she was saying. Dad just turned his face away and sat in silence. As if not acknowledging the facts – or her feelings – would make them go away. Mom laid on the guilt thick, like spreading butter on toast. 'This is *not* the future we imagined for our kids when we migrated to America in 1986 …' she began.

'I know,' interrupted Leela. 'Everything you did, you did it for our good. But who decides what is good? You didn't let me be a normal American teenager. No matter how hard I tried, I could never fit in. There were too many unwritten rules. Like, dating is allowed once you are in college. With a nice Indian boy, if possible. But under no circumstances, should you fall for one of "those people".'

As she lay in the heat, Leela found herself thinking about Raymond. Her boyfriend for seven months in college.

He was tall, dark and handsome, and was pursuing an engineering degree. But the look on her parents' faces when she introduced him to them was that of complete shock and disappointment. That look haunted her for many weeks and, anyway, it was a college romance. Why let it get serious? They broke up before graduating and had not been in touch since.

Leela's reverie was broken by a man in uniform taking off her handcuffs.

'We are really sorry, miss; we didn't know you are from the press. This was a mistake,' said Officer Delpatrick.

Leela blinked and looked around. Scores of protesters were still on the ground, their hands restrained with plastic zip ties. For there were not enough handcuffs.

No force in the world strong enough to perpetuate The Lie.

***

The 2022 Pulitzer Prize winners in journalism and seven other categories were announced online. There was a special citation at the bottom of the list. It read: 'Leelavathi Natarajan: For her outstanding and courageous reporting on #BlackLivesMatter.'

That afternoon, there was a 'follow request' on Instagram. Raymond Samson, lead engineer at Google – looking handsome as ever. And still single …

As she clicked on 'accept', Leela felt her heart beating faster. After a long, long time.

Rishtey Naatey

Ankit glanced at the clock on the corner of his screen and wondered why time was moving so slowly. It felt like the Zoom meeting had gone on forever. Everyone – except the speaker – was slyly checking their phones. Like the art of listening to lectures with your eyes open and brain shut, this was a newly acquired skill in the pandemic.

ping

Ankit opened the WhatsApp notification.

'Tata launched its shopping site. Please use this instead of Amazon or other Chinese site.'

'There goes mamaji again,' thought Ankit. 'First of all, this Tata shopping site has been around for at least three years now. Secondly ... Ab kya kahein? Jab se mamaji Allahabad High Court se retire hue hain, family WhatsApp group mein apna raub jhaad rahe hain. He has knowledge of some things, but an opinion on everything.'

Ankit's mind went into overdrive.

'On our family group, the day starts with a devotional photo shared by Sudha mausiji. That's her one and only daily contribution. Someone will reply "Jai mata di", followed by a dozen messages with the namaste emoji. Though originally created as a high five, we Indians have nicely adapted it as per apna requirement. Go, India, go.

'In a single day, mamaji covers more topics than Arnab Goswami – from the state of the economy to the state of the world. The only thing we are spared are his bowel movements. He is against stray dogs, cold food, delivery charges and Arvind Kejriwal. I have half a mind to exit this group, but then, who will keep track of birthdays? Besides, there is something called respect for elders.'

His reverie was broken by another message. 'Yaar, isi liye to hum mamaji ko kuch keh nahin paatey,' grumbled Guarav, his cousin, in their private chat.

Ankit thought of the wedding in Udaipur they had attended recently. Following the ladies' sangeet, there was an impromptu mehfil. Which brought out the *other* side of mamaji. Urdu sher-o-shayari, a purana shauk from his student days at the University of Allahabad. Suddenly, you could imagine him in a bandhgala with a rose in hand. A kinder, gentler, younger man.

After making sure the oldies were fast asleep, the cousins sat around the terrace with a bottle of Old Monk to keep themselves warm. And Gaurav finally got drunk enough to blurt out, 'Yaar, ek baat batao. Yun to mamaji har waqt Ram Rajya waale forwards daalte hain ... By that logic, he should be reciting Sanskrit poetry. Kal farmaaish karte hain.'

The cousins all laughed as if the best joke in the world had just been cracked. Naturally, no one had the guts to actually say anything to mamaji, but the next day, at lunch and at dinner, the younger lot had a private joke to laugh about.

On the flight back to Mumbai, Ankit accompanied Sudha mausiji, who was travelling alone. And that was when he got to know the real story. Mamaji had fallen in love with a Muslim girl in college. Both sets of parents had opposed the match fiercely. The girl was married off post-haste, while lovelorn mamaji expressed his gham by writing couplets.

'Pitaji ne phir ek din bula kar zor se daaanta – yeh kya naatak chal raha hai?' Sudha mausiji told Ankit.

The next morning, mamaji shaved off his stubble and started preparing for his law exams. He passed the bar and got married.

'But kabhi donon ki aapas mein bani nahin,' mausiji confided in Ankit. 'Toh bas, they lived together under the same roof, but apart.' Mamaji in the court, mamiji in the club. Until retirement, when suddenly, there was nothing to do, nowhere to escape ...

Ankit blinked as he noticed his colleagues leaving the meeting. How little he knew of the man behind the mamaji tag.

***

Two years later

The Netflix series *Rishtey Naatey* opened to rave reviews. Reviewers were all praise for Ankit Agrawal, the writer of the series, who quit his job at Deloitte to work on the compelling script.

'My own family was the inspiration behind this saga spanning three generations,' he said in interviews.

For once, everyone agreed when mamaji posted the clapping emoji for Ankit on the WhatsApp group.

And Ankit replied with a genuine smiley.

Work Is Worship

Abdul Khan wiped the drop of sweat trickling down his brow. After the pleasant month of March, temperatures were beginning to rise again in Delhi. But it was nowhere as bad as his native village in Uttar Pradesh. Bhai wahan ki toh garmi ki baat hi kuch aur hai. Aur wahan ke aam ki bhi. His mouth watered at the memory.

'Which world are you lost in?' snapped the supervisor. 'Focus on your work!'

Abdul was startled out of his reverie. His fingers had momentarily stopped sewing buttons. Mentally, he kicked himself. This job was precious – he could not afford to lose it. Never mind if his eyes were tired or fingers stiff. Living like this, so far away from home and family, was not his choice. But he was determined to make it out of here. With something to show for it.

Ammi jaan had begged him not to leave. He did look, quite desperately, for a job near his village. Any job. But what decent option is available in such a backward area? There are government schemes like MNREGA, but should a Class 12-pass like him be doing sadak banane ka kaam? What was the point of passing exams, getting an education?

It was then that he decided that sheher toh jaana padega. He would earn enough every month to send something back home. 'Anyway,' he reasoned to himself, 'if that useless Babban Sheikh could do it, why not me?'

Reluctantly, ammi gave him dua, dawa and khaane ka dabba. And off he went, in an unreserved compartment of an Indian Railways coach, towards destination Dilli.

And here he was, two years later. Things had not quite worked out the way Abdul had wanted. He wasn't doing a job worthy of a graduate. But he had three square meals a day and a roof over his head.

'Hamesha achha socho,' Ammi used to tell him. And that's what kept Abdul going.

This job, in which he had to sit and do mindless work for hours, was something to be grateful for. The sookhi roti and dal he ate for lunch day after day, which had no taste, kept him alive. The image of Nazneen in a white salwar–kameez, the girl he secretly liked and hoped to marry someday, brought solace in his worst moments. When he wanted to run away from this place ...

'Abdul!' barked the supervisor again.

His co-workers stared as Abdul walked out of the karkhaana, down the corridor, to madam's office. She was a legendary figure – not many had a chance to meet her personally. Abdul considered himself lucky. 'Besides,' he willed himself, 'jab maine koi galat kaam kiya hi nahi, toh darna kyun?' When he was ushered in to the large office, he looked madam in the eye with confidence.

She was poring over some papers, but looked up and met his gaze. And she liked what she saw. A young man with no fear, no insolence. His work record was impeccable – no rowdy behaviour, always exceeding his targets. Managing human resources was a huge challenge. This one had a spark of potential ...

It was a tough job, giving these angry young men some sense of agency, some hope. Often, it failed, but she kept trying anyway.

'Abdul, tumhara kaam acchha hai aur padhe–likhe bhi ho. We have a new job in mind for you.'

It was in an adjacent unit, which made snacks and potato chips. Abdul would be in charge of the production diary – recording the wastage of potatoes, the number of bags of chips sealed per day, and all other data pertaining to the snacks factory. This would be in addition to working on the assembly line, so it was extra effort. With only slightly more pay.

But Abdul was happy. It was a sign of progress! 'Kisi na kisi din achhe din aayenge,' was his first thought. 'I will go back to the village, to my Ammi jaan. To Nazneen. Till then I will survive. Inshallah.'

***

In April 2020, Abdul was released from Tihar jail, on emergency parole, along with 4,000 undertrials. Thanks to the Covid-19 scare.

'Don't do anything stupid,' madam warned them. 'Go home, get some rest, stay in quarantine, enjoy this time with your family.'

Abdul knew he would do just that. He could waste his life plotting revenge against the seth who had falsely implicated him, or serve his time and start afresh.

For unlike the majority, Abdul had already made his escape. From the most powerful prison in the world – the prison of the mind.

Tell Me Why

Naina was never allowed to watch *MasterChef Australia*. Oh, how wonderful everything was about that show, about that kitchen. And those three roly-poly judges. It was Naina's dream to, one day, be a contestant on that show. But in her heart, she knew it wasn't possible. Born into a strict Jain household, she had never eaten eggs, meat or fish. And that was just the start of it.

'How can you live without onion, garlic *and* potato?' her best friend, Rhea, always wondered.

Strange and wonderful smells would waft out of her tiffin box. But Rhea ignored that and was always more excited about Naina's dabba. She was crazy about Mumma's kachoris, parathas, dhoklas ... All the stuff Naina was sick and tired of. While other girls had dreams about Ranbir Kapoor, she dreamt of eating a proper samosa one day.

Not one stuffed with kachcha kela. Or moong dal. Or cabbage. Just potato, the humble brown spud, growing just beneath the ground. The Jain munis said this was to prevent the destruction of microorganisms ... But why was the whole world's burden of 'ahimsa' on the shoulders this group of people who represented just 0.3 per cent of India's population?

All the youth camps she had attended at the ashram did not provide satisfactory answers to this question. But well, there was more to life than food. Naina was an excellent student; she topped her school as well as her college. Finally, pappa gave her his permission to pursue her Master's degree abroad. And she secured admission to the London School of Economics.

'But how will you manage there? What will you eat?' was mumma's main concern.

After extensive research done through WhatsApp family and friend's groups, mumma drew out a 'safe list' of all the things Naina could possibly buy in supermarkets or restaurants in London. 'But best to look for an Indian store, haan?' was her mother's advice. She also enrolled Naina to Nita Jain's crash course on cooking, formulated especially for Indian students overseas.

Actually, Naina had entirely different plans. 'The minute I land in the UK, I am going to eat whatever the hell I want. All the stuff I haven't eaten for the last twenty-three years of my life. Nobody knows, nobody gets hurt,' she told herself.

And that is exactly what she would have done, had it not been for her roommate, Alma, who was from Germany.

The very first day they moved into their dorm, Alma had visited the supermarket and stocked up on all kinds of fruits and vegetables. She put them into a blender with some nuts and seeds, and drank the concoction for dinner. It wasn't a milkshake with milk, but a smoothie. Made with something called 'almond milk'. 'Ab doodh mein badam toh suna tha, par badam se doodh banta hai?' Naina wondered.

'I am vegan,' explained Alma. 'I don't have any dairy products.'

'How can you live without butter, ghee *and* cheese?' thought Naina. But over the next two months, she learnt ki yeh sab ho sakta hai. Alma made light and tasty meals, using all kinds of herbs and interesting sauces. And she was absolutely delighted to eat the food Naina gingerly prepared, even if it was simple dal–chawal.

When they hosted a Christmas party together, Naina served Haldiram's ready-made pani puri (Indian store zindabad!), while Alma made a delicious sizzling brownie (no one could tell it was vegan!). The guests could not stop raving about how amazing the food was. Naina and Alma looked at each other, and smiled.

'Let's start a petition online for a new season of *MasterChef* – no meat, no fish, no dairy, no eggs. And every possible dish that can be made with raw banana!' Naina said.

***

Two years later

A new diet is taking the world by storm. It involves simple ideas like eating before sunset and 'intermittent fasting', or not eating for twelve to fourteen hours. This amuses Naina.

'My grandmother is a strict Jain and she has been following this diet for the last sixty-five years!' she tells Alma.

The wisdom of the ages is contained in the fabric of our daily lives. If only we can explain the science behind it and follow it, with our heads held high.

Bachpan ke Din

Sonali was dreading 13 June. It was her fiftieth birthday, which felt like a Really Big One. Over the past year, her friends had done such exotic celebrations – in Phuket and Bali. That wasn't Sonali's plan, but still, she felt cheated. With this endless lockdown, she didn't even have a *choice* now, did she?

'I still remember your birthday parties,' said her childhood friend, Roopali. If only they could all go back to those carefree days …

Those birthdays were grand occasions when they got to eat all their favourite foods. Stuff their faces with samosa, wafers, chutney sandwiches and cake. All made at home, except for the wafers, which had to come from 'Victory', the famous shop along 1st Pasta Lane. And the birthday girl got to pick out the Gems of her choice from the cake! What could be cooler than that?

They played games like 'passing the parcel', 'pin the tail on the donkey' and 'four continents'. Also the 'memory game' – which was too serious for Sonali's liking – but hey, four games were a must! At the end of the party, the birthday girl got to tear open the presents. Though, Sonali remembered, Mummy always reminded her to open them gently (for wrapping paper must always be reused!).

The best possible gift one could receive was a set of Amar Chitra Kathas (which cost a princely Rs 3 per copy). Whoops of joy, for new titles had come home at last. Or sighs of disappointment, for repeats and bores. And these books were kept in mint condition to be passed on to the next birthday girl on the calendar. Poor 'Tukaram', nobody wanted him ... Sonali remembered that he came back to her after a whole cycle of 'passing the gift around'.

'Who knew those days would end so quickly?' Sonali mused.

You grow up together, play together, laugh and cry together, and then one day, you just drift apart. The gulf between continents, of responsibilities, of children to bring up, and ambitions at work – they all take their toll. And husbands, too. No matter how great a guy you marry, it is never enough. He doesn't know the six-year-old you, the twelve-year-old-you, the eighteen-year-old you.

The girl behind the woman.

That evening, Sonali pulled out all an old album from her childhood and relived the memories. A memorable thirteenth birthday party – in pink pedal pushers, bought from Inter-Shoppe at Kemps Corner. Her first-ever 'dance party' – where Nazia and Zoheb Hassan ruled. Everyone looking so young and innocent, and *slim*. Weight loss was not yet a thing in their lives.

On her usual nightly call with her daughter, a freshman at Boston University, Sonali shared these purani yaadein. Mitali had never heard her mom talk with such nostalgia about the Railway Colony in which she grew up. The gossiping, sleepovers, Dalgona coffee ('We were making it long before it got fashionable!'). It was all too fascinating for Mitali … She hung on to every word.

'Mom! You made a blank call to a guy you had a crush on? Tell me more!' she gasped.

But moms, you know. They love to go back to mundane topics of discussion. Are you eating properly? Wear your mask! What about groceries? 'Gosh, when will she stop worrying about me,' Mitali wondered.

But then a thought struck her.

***

On 13 June, at 8 a.m. IST, Sonali saw messages from Roopali and Mitali with a Zoom link.

'SURPRISE!' It was Vandana and Manisha, Rashmi, Shefali, Deepali, Sujata, Pradnya, Shalini, Shivani, Rekha, Anu, Tanu, Tehseen, Melo, Anuradha, Kavita, Lalita, Reema, Geeta, Girija and Deepa. All her childhood friends had gathered together once again to celebrate Sonali's birthday.

There were no samosas or cake or presents. But just being together. It was the greatest gift of all.

Mission Impossible

The mountain air is crisp, the sky a brilliant blue. Michael Pendegrast is in awe, drinking it all in. The Yosemite and Yellowstone National Parks, where he loves to go hiking and rock-climbing, are pygmies when compared to these green valleys and majestic mountains. But, lurking under the surface of this paradise, is the darkness of greed and politics.

'We are freedom fighters,' Hameed tells him, a young man in his twenties, an active member of the Liberation Front.

Growing up, Hameed felt 'different' from the rest of his countrymen. His grandfather and his father were both secret supporters of azaadi. Meetings were often held in their home, on the pretext of a daawat. Fragrant pulao would be served along with lamb stew, but the real agenda was where to procure weapons from and how to enlist more young men in the Resistance.

Every year, in the month of August, Hameed's school celebrated 'Independence Day' – which was when they had got freedom from British rule. But, to this little boy, the flag that fluttered that day was not his flag. He refused to salute it and earned a reprimand. Hameed came home that day with a mark on his face where the headmaster had slapped him.

And, on that day, another freedom fighter was born.

No one wants to bring up their children in an atmosphere of violence and hatred. But, sometimes, there is no choice. When your home, which enjoys the bounty of nature, is exploited by outsiders. When it becomes a pawn in the hands of greedy politicians. When people in the mainland do not understand who you are ...

'I want a better future for *my* children,' says Hameed. A future he knows he may never live to see.

Hameed's wife, Bushra, is a delicate woman with long black hair and green eyes. She is only nineteen, but is expecting their second child. Living in this strife-torn and underdeveloped region, Bushra didn't get a chance to complete her schooling. The reporter in Michael wonders what she feels about her husband's dangerous obsession with azaadi. But he wisely keeps his mouth shut.

When Michael set out for this assignment, his editor had warned him not to judge the people he met through the lens of Western cultural values. As an undercover reporter, he would be dealing with many challenges. The last thing he wanted was to do is antagonize his contacts. Things could get tricky and even the Consulate might not be able to help …

It is the month of May, when the snow is melting and the brooks are gurgling. This is an excellent time to strike. Hameed and his fellow fighters are planning something big. An attack on an army convoy.

To inflict maximum damage, they plan to ram a truck with improvised explosive devices (IEDs) into the convoy. The more soldiers killed, the bigger the news headline.

Michael watches as Hameed says his final goodbyes to his family. His eyes are determined and they are dry. Bushra watches him from a distance; her face betraying no emotions. It is Hameed's two-year-old son who runs after his father, tugging at his pajama, imploring him not to go. The fighter lifts the little boy up and holds him in his arms for what seems like an eternity.

Gently, he puts the boy down at last and wipes away his child's tears, and his own.

'Be strong for your mother,' says Hameed, and then, he is gone.

That night, Michael is unable to sleep; he is waiting for the news. As he tosses and turns, he wonders, 'Is it worth the pain and the sacrifice? How many more must die in vain?'

There are no answers, only more and more questions.

***

Two days later

Six Pakistani soldiers were killed in a deadly attack on an army convoy by members of the Balochistan Liberation Front.

GEO TV reports, 'The prime minister of Pakistan has blamed a foreign hand. India denies any involvement.'

In a small village, in the Sulaiman Mountains, a young woman is now a widow. And yet another freedom fighter is born.

Workshop Stories

By students of Rashmi Bansal's short-story writing programme

And That's the Way the Cookie Crumbled

Devakee Rahalkar

'Just one hour more,' Juhi muttered to herself as she tried to get up from her seat yet again, in an effort to end one of the most boring meetings of her life. Her clients finally seemed to be done with their lengthy last-minute directives and were saying their goodbyes.

It had been a long day at the end of a tiring week and Juhi was exhausted. Having sat through continuous meetings since the morning, she was done with her quota of talking to people. She was happily looking forward to entering the sanctum of her small one-bedroom flat, ordering some comfort food, a long, hot shower and bingeing on her new favourite series on Netflix.

Just forty minutes more and she would be home!

Juhi dashed to her car via the back door to avoid a cluster of her co-workers who were stepping out for a drink. She stopped by her neighbourhood grocery store to stock up on junk food for the weekend. She was careful to look down and not meet anyone's eye, lest she run into an acquaintance and invite pointless chit-chat.

Juhi knew she could seem like an odd duck to some. A classic introvert, she routinely took extreme measures to avoid social interactions. She was happy to talk to strangers if it involved her work and loved spending quality time with a few chosen friends. It was the big parties, making small talk and new introductions that she found mentally draining.

Her lack of a social life was a constant source of worry for her mother, but Juhi was not too keen to change her hermit lifestyle.

Almost there! Another five minutes and she could step out of her high heels onto the soft carpet of her home. Just as Juhi was exiting the elevator, her phone trilled. Expecting it to be the daily call from her mother, she swiped up.

'Its FRIIIIDAY!', Lata, her best friend since school, shrieked into the phone. Juhi groaned, cursing herself for not screening her calls.

'I have had a hellish week and you are coming out with me. It is a done deal! You cannot avoid every Friday-evening ran a brush through her hair and grabbed her wallet to make a quick trip to the pastry shop.

'After an entire week of healthy eating and demanding clients, I need that pastry!' she reasoned on the drive to 10th Road.

Entering the bakery, Juhi stood by the counter, taking in all the delicacies. Everything looked so good, she could barely decide what to order.

'I would recommend the Oreo cookie crumble,' a deep voice behind her said.

She straightened up to look for the source of this unsolicited advice, and found herself looking into a pair of warm, twinkling brown eyes.

'Oh my god, Adi!' Juhi gasped, recognizing her old friend.

Pulling her into a tight hug, Adi beamed down at Juhi. She felt a burst of joy seeing that familiar grin again.

Juhi knew Adi had moved back to Mumbai recently, but had not made an effort to reach out. Juhi and Adi had been very close during the last three years at school. She even had a crush on him back then, and had always idly wondered if it had been anything worth exploring. But they moved to different cities for their higher studies and subsequent jobs, and had lost touch over the last decade.

In their years apart, Adi had grown from a tall, lanky boy into an extremely attractive man. Juhi was thankful that she had made an effort to wear her favourite jeans and at least comb her hair before stepping out.

outing,' Lata prattled on without giving Juhi a chance to refuse. She knew her friend's introverted tendencies too well.

'Sorry, I have a hot date with Netflix, pizza and some chocolate,' Juhi countered, as she entered her flat and collapsed on her sofa.

'You are twenty-eight. Single. You need to go out and interact with flesh-and-blood human beings before your mother gets serious about opening that matrimonial profile,' Lata admonished her.

'You need to stop gossiping with my mother. And I haven't met anyone recently who is yummier than Captain Ri on Netflix!'

'I was planning to explore that new bakery on 10th Road tonight with some friends – the one with those delicious, drool-worthy pastries in the window,' said Lata. Juhi knew what Lata was doing; she was exploiting her greatest weakness – chocolate desserts.

'Um …,' Juhi briefly considered going out with Lata, but then she sank into her sofa and knew she wouldn't get out anytime soon. She pleaded out.

Three hours later, after gorging on pepperoni pizza and wrapping up another season of her favourite K-drama, Juhi picked up her phone to scroll through Instagram.

'Damn it, Lata!', she muttered as she saw her friend post a photo of a delicious-looking chocolate pastry, the tag indicating the bakery on 10th Road.

Fifteen minutes later, the picture of that chocolate pastry was still on Juhi's mind. She reluctantly pulled on her jeans,

All her weariness forgotten, she was excited to catch up with Adi once again. They sat in the café with their coffees and an Oreo cookie crumble between them – exchanging stories and laughing over old memories late into the night.

Juhi woke up with a smile the next morning. Adi was single, funny and was clearly interested in her. They had planned a lunch date later in the day and she was excited that she had finally met someone who was interested in her.

Wanting to share this foreign feeling with her best friend, she dialled Lata's number. A pre-recorded message in Kannada told her Lata's phone was busy.

'Strange!' she thought.

Lata often travelled to Bengaluru for work, but hadn't she called last night with an offer to hang out? And had she not posted a photo from the same café a few hours before Juhi?

Her phone pinged with a text from Lata, 'Call you in sometime.'

'Where are you?! Did you not get back from Bengaluru this week?' Juhi responded.

'Busted! I hope the conversation around Oreo cookie crumble was worth all my hard work.'

'You are such a liar!' Juhi was astounded by her friend's elaborate scheme to fabricate a dream date for her.

'Yes, but a bloody brilliant one. That is why you love me,' came the reply promptly.

'Yes, I do love you. THANK YOU! You are the best! X'

Smiling, Juhi sent a quick prayer of thanks and got out of bed. She had a lunch date to get ready for.

The Witness

Bhuvaneswari Mathuraiveeran

🌀

'Mummy, look what I made today!' Aadya came running to show her newly made card. It had sunflowers, mountains, the sun and her favourite Baloo.

Anu looked at the picture and smiled broadly. 'Beautiful, kuttu!'

Aadya ran to get her teddy, Baloo; the two were inseparable. Anu made a mental note to put the raggedy toy into the washing machine.

Aadya was talking to Baloo. 'I am meeting Vikrant this Saturday; we will play all evening. Baloo, do you want to come?'

Anu jumped in and said, 'No, Baloo will be at home and will guard the house.'

Aadya was super happy to be going to someone's house after three long months. Thanks to Covid-19 and lockdowns, she had been rather lonely.

Rahul peered out of his home office. 'What are you people up to?' he asked his wife and daughter.

Aadya ran to Rahul and sat on his lap. 'Papa. Let us play!'

This was the frequent dialogue at home nowadays. Anu dreamt of the 'normal days' when she would actually go back to office.

The preparations to go to Vikrant's house were on. Anu was busy baking cookies, Rahul had ordered some wine and Aadya was drawing another card to be handed over. This one had a 'welcome' banner, three stick figures inside the house and three stick-figure visitors, with Baloo standing a little away.

As they were leaving the house, Anu noticed that Aadya was clutching Baloo tightly.

'No, kuttu. I've told you before; you can't take him along!'

But Aadya refused to listen. Finally, Rahul had to intervene.

'It's only a teddy bear, yaar. Let her carry it. Come on, we're getting late!'

Half an hour later, they were standing outside a door bearing the name 'Mehras'.

'Welcome! So glad to see you ... We've been planning this for so long. And who is *this*?' Vikrant's father bent down and spoke to Aadya.

'This is Baloo!' said Aadya, shyly.

'Ah, welcome to Baloo and to this cute little girl as well,' said Ravi Mehra.

The evening went better than expected. Vikrant's mother was a superb cook, while his father was an entertainer. He kept all of them engaged the whole evening. After mixing drinks for the adults, Ravi whipped up some mocktails for the kids.

'What does Aadya like – orange or pineapple juice?'

While the grown-ups were gossiping, he took it upon himself to see what the bachcha party was up to.

'Wish Rahul was so thoughtful!' Anu couldn't help musing.

The kids were fast asleep and it was past 1 a.m. when they finally got up to leave. But not before making a plan to meet again the following weekend.

A couple of days later, Aadya asked, 'Mom, why does Ravi uncle have moustache? And why does papa not have one?'

Anu answered absent-mindedly, 'Papa likes to be clean-shaven, kuttu.'

'Is Ravi uncle a monster? The moustache is scary, isn't it, Mom?'

Anu looked at Aadya, 'It's a personal choice, kuttu. Uncle might like it; hence, he keeps it. Why is it bothering you?'

Aadya didn't answer, but started concentrating on her drawing instead. Anu felt a little concerned, but let it go.

The next morning, while cleaning the living room, Anu found a drawing with not just Baloo but a figure with a moustache standing in the dark.

She showed it to her husband. 'Rahul, look at this drawing Aadya made. That figure with a moustache is not looking right to me.'

Rahul glanced at the drawing and shrugged as if to say, 'Women and their overactive imaginations!'

The following weekend, Vikrant's family visited Aadya's home. Ravi was a charmer once again – helping Anu in the kitchen and letting his wife relax.

'Aadya is such a sweet kid,' remarked Ravi. Anu nodded, but did not reply.

Once again, he offered to look into what the kids were up to. But Anu was uncomfortable this time, and she couldn't quite put her finger on it …

'Hey, you are a guest in our home. Relax, I'll take care of it,' she said, preparing a tray with some juice, chips and dip for the kids.

Ravi wasn't his usual gregarious self for the rest of the evening. Even the socially clueless Rahul noticed this change.

'Was the wine not good enough?' he asked when the guests departed at 10 p.m. Anu was lost in thought.

As she tucked Aadya into bed that night, she wondered whether it was the right time to bring up an important topic.

'Not now; I will do it tomorrow,' she told herself.

Summoning all her courage, the next morning, she had the talk.

'Kuttu, you know, na, that no one is allowed to touch your chest, your bum, your lips or anywhere near your susu place.

If anyone does that you, just shout or run out of that place and then tell Mama. Clear, kuttu?' Aadya nodded diligently.

The next card Aadya drew was for Rahul's birthday. In that one too, there was a figure with a moustache watching them.

Anu could not contain herself this time.

'Aadya, who is this person in the drawing next to Baloo?'

Aadya looked around and said in a very low voice, 'Mom. It is a secret.'

'Beta, no secrets with Mom; you know that. Why don't you tell me?'

Aadya was tense. She came close and whispered in her ear, 'Mom, Ravi uncle asked me to keep this secret. He said he will be watching me always, like Baloo …'

Till We Meet Again

Rengarajan T.S.

'Raghu, this is impossible. Bruno is afflicted with arthritis, but he has a lot of life left in him! Forget it!' said the veterinarian.

Raghu looked deep into the eyes of Dr Kulkarni and repeated, 'Please, do it. Do it for my sake.'

Waiting for Kulkarni to finish attending to one more dog, Raghu started ruminating. Ten years ago, on a chilly December morning, as he went on his daily walk, he found a tiny puppy near Bandstand whining away.

Unable to control himself, Raghu bent down and asked, 'How are you? Why are you crying? Did you lose your mother?'

The puppy wagged its tail and got up, but continued to whine. Raghu thought he might be hungry, but no shops were open yet. He sighed and walked away.

A few steps down, he noticed that the puppy was following him. Twice, he tried to shoo him away but the puppy was unrelenting.

Raghu stopped, bent down, looked at the puppy said, 'You can't come with me. My wife doesn't like dogs'.

The puppy seemed to be least bothered by this fact. It started licking his feet. Raghu couldn't resist; he picked up the puppy and went home.

Sheela opened the door and was shocked to see Raghu holding a puppy in his arms.

'What is this, Raghu? You know I don't like dogs!' she exclaimed.

'I know, but let's give him some milk, ma; he's hungry,' replied Raghu.

Reluctantly, Sheela brought out some milk in a coconut shell. The little one drank the milk in a few gulps and looked up at his benefactor lovingly. Sheela went into the kitchen murmuring something about taking him away immediately, as it might be difficult later.

'Let me have a bath first,' Raghu told her, leaving the puppy in the balcony.

Sheela was busy preparing breakfast, but she suddenly felt something wet on her feet – the puppy was busy licking her feet. She was terribly angry, and shouted at both the puppy and Raghu. The puppy ran and hid behind the kitchen door.

A few minutes later, as she set the table for breakfast, she noticed the puppy still standing behind the door.

He looked so small and vulnerable. And soon, he would be back on the road …

Sheela returned to the kitchen and tried to focus on making the filter coffee. 'Really,' she reasoned to herself, 'one can't take in every stray animal … There are just too many in this world!'

After having his breakfast, Raghu stood up. 'Sheela, I am going out to leave this guy somewhere and will be back soon.'

Sheela saw Raghu standing by the door with the puppy. The little guy was snuggled in the old man's arms. What a helpless little baby.

After a pause, Sheela said, 'Let Bruno stay.'

Raghu looked askance at Sheela. 'Are you sure?'

She nodded, lump in throat. Gosh, she must be getting sentimental with age.

'Okay, little man! I see you already have a name,' said Raghu, pleased as punch.

Bruno soon became a part of the family. The couple's children lived in the US and were instantly won over by the four-legged furball when they came visiting.

It wasn't long before Bruno's name was added to the wooden nameplate outside their door.

But if happy tidings come in a spate, so do unhappy tidings. Bruno developed arthritis. He couldn't walk much and was in a lot of pain. He was being treated by Dr Kulkarni.

Soon after, Sheela noticed a lump in her breast. It was diagnosed as malignant.

All of a sudden, life changed. Raghu didn't know how to handle the situation. It was difficult to hold back his tears while giving Sheela false assurances of everything being all right soon.

Bruno was his constant companion when he stood in the balcony, weeping. The dog seemed to understand Raghu's agony. He tried to comfort Sheela as well, by nuzzling up against her whenever he got the chance.

Finally, the end came.

Sheela passed away.

The children came down to help their father and, before leaving, they requested him to join them for some time, to get over the loneliness. Raghu had no other option. He had never ever thought of life without Sheela. He now had to find a home for sick Bruno.

Dr Kulkarni suggested that Raghu leave Bruno in a farm in Panvel, belonging to his friend. Over the next few nights, Raghu would often get up and find Bruno writhing in pain. He would then softly massage Bruno's legs, comforting him. Until the poor animal finally fell asleep.

Raghu finally made up his mind.

'Kulkarni, let's put Bruno to sleep,' he said. 'I can't live with the thought of him suffering so much and that too without me.'

Dr Kulkarni was initially reluctant, but when Raghu refused to reconsider, he had no choice. He prepared the injection to put Bruno to sleep permanently.

For one last time, he asked, 'Raghu, are you sure you want to do this?'

'Yes,' said Raghu, even as he broke down and sobbed like a baby. Bruno was licking his feet, unable to see his master cry.

Raghu held Bruno in his arms one last time and whispered into his ears, 'Very soon you will be with Sheela aai. She will take care of you.'

Bruno wagged his tail and gave a gentle woof, as he closed his eyes. Forever.

Flying High

Srivatsan G.

❧

'LADIES AND GENTLEMEN, WE ARE EXPERIENCING SOME turbulence. The captain has turned on the fasten seat belt sign. Please return to your seats and keep your seat belts fastened. Thank you,' sounded the PA of United Airlines Flight, UA 867 from San Francisco to New Delhi.

Suresh, who was engrossed in the financial section of the *New York Times*, kept the paper down and fastened his seat belt.

'As if I don't have enough turbulence in my life already!'

The last few months had been really tough on him and his team. As head of the artificial intelligence vertical at Google,

Suresh had been grappling with various anti-trust lawsuits by multiple regulatory agencies. The decision to fly home had been an impulsive one – he badly needed a break.

Chanting 'Om Namah Shivaya', he hoped for the turbulence to pass.

After an eventful ten minutes, it was announced that the flight was 'comfortably cruising'. Suresh opened the window shade and looked at the faint feathery clouds outside.

His mind wandered …

Suresh was born and brought up in a small village near Trichy, Tamil Nadu. His father, Krishnan, worked in a flour mill and was the sole breadwinner of the family. He had taken huge loans to marry off his eldest daughter and had struggled to make ends meet.

Suresh was a studious young boy and showed a lot of interest in learning new things.

'Which weighs more – a ton of concrete or a ton of feathers? Can anyone tell me?' Ramu Sir asked the Class 8 students. There was pin-drop silence. Just when Ramu sir was about to leave, Suresh raised his hands and answered, 'They both weigh the same, sir; a ton.'

Ramu Sir patted his back and left the class.

Suresh was not seen in class for the next couple of days. Days turned into weeks and Suresh remained absent. No one had any clue as to why he was missing. Perhaps he was sick? It was then that Ramu Sir decided to visit Suresh's house and find out for himself.

One evening, after school, he reached the address listed in the school records. The student's home was just a thatched hut. Ramu Sir called out for Suresh a couple of times, but there was no reply. Finally, a frail lady with a creased forehead came out and asked, 'Who are you? What do you want?'

Ramu Sir greeted her and said, 'I am Suresh's science teacher.'

'He is not at home. He has gone to work with his father,' the lady replied.

'No problem, I shall wait then,' said Ramu Sir. He sat on the mud verandah outside. It was around 8 p.m. when Suresh returned, looking sad and tired.

He was startled to see his teacher at his doorstep.

'What happened, thambi? Why are you not attending school for the last one month?' questioned the teacher.

Suresh simply looked at his father.

'What is the point in educating him when we are unable to manage our household?' retorted Krishnan.

Suresh was earning Rs 500 a month and that was a decent enough contribution for a struggling family.

'But, sir, your son is one of the brightest students in the entire school. If you allow him to continue his studies, he will have an excellent future.'

'Who cares about the future when our current survival is uncertain?' asked Krishnan bluntly. Ramu Sir left without furthering the discussion.

The next day, the teacher paid another visit to Suresh's house.

'Why are you troubling us?' snapped Krishnan. 'I told you clearly yesterday that we are not interested in continuing his studies.'

Ramu Sir calmly responded, 'The Lions Club of Trichy is ready to offer a scholarship for his studies and, additionally, pay him Rs 1,000 every month if he accepts our proposal.'

'Which is?' Krishnan was now interested.

'He will be paid Rs 1,000 every month if he agrees to continue his education and spend three hours a day in the school library as a part-time librarian in the evenings. Our regular librarian leaves at 5 p.m. and we need someone till 8 p.m.'

Krishnan's face lit up like a 100-watt bulb. He readily accepted the proposal. Ramu Sir was delighted to see Suresh back in class the next day. That evening, as he was leaving school, Ramu Sir saw Suresh reading *The Evolution of Physics* by Albert Einstein in the library.

The teacher beamed with joy.

Suresh's reverie was broken by the flight attendant asking, 'Sir, would you like to have a cup of hot tea?'

While sipping on his tea, he decided that he would definitely visit his school this time and meet Ramu Sir.

The connecting flight from Delhi to Chennai was delayed. It was 2 a.m. by the time he finally reached his lavish three-bedroom home in the heart of Chennai. The next morning, Suresh woke up at 6 a.m. and prepared to leave for Trichy.

'Thambi, please take rest,' his father urged him. 'You didn't sleep properly. You can visit the school a couple of days later.'

Suresh replied with a smile, 'Illa Appa, it's been twenty years since I visited my school. Rest can take a back seat today.'

Ramu Sir was now the principal of Government Higher Secondary School, Trichy. His secretary, Rosario, requested Suresh to wait outside his room.

'Principal sir should be back in five minutes,' he informed.

When Ramu Sir returned, Suresh got up from his chair and instinctively bowed down to touch his feet. The teacher had aged considerably, with thick glasses covering his dark-circled eyes, and he needed a walking stick for support. He was bewildered, as there had been no visitors scheduled for the day.

'Sir, he claims to be your old student, Suresh,' briefed Rosario.

'Which Suresh?' wondered Ramu Sir.

'Part-time evening librarian Suresh,' came the reply, with a wide smile. Ramu Sir came forward and hugged him immediately.

The conversation between guru and shishya went on for the next one hour. It was interrupted only when Rosario knocked on the door and said, 'Sir, Class 10 students are waiting for your science class.' Suresh bid adieu to his guru with a heavy heart.

The next day was the annual sports day of the school and Ramu Sir was busy making preparations for the event. Rosario tapped on his door.

'Sir, sorry to disturb you. This was given by Mr Suresh yesterday.'

It was a shiny new envelope with a letter inside.

Dear sir,

Without you, I would be nothing today. The scholarship and Rs 1,000 each month made a big difference in my life, which can't be expressed in words. From Trichy to IIT Madras to Google, California – my life has been a roller coaster. For all that you have done for me, here is a small token of love.

Ramu Sir was startled to see a cheque for Rs 25 lakh attached with the letter. He had never seen such a huge amount in his life before. As tears welled up in his eyes, he noticed a tiny yellow note pasted on the back of the cheque.

I knew from the beginning that it was you who sponsored my education, not the Lions Club. You seemed to have forgotten the fact that Ganesh, my best friend in school, was the day-time librarian's son.
  What a lie, sir, but a brilliant one – definitely much better than all the defence Google is putting up against the anti-trust lawsuits!

Love and pranaam,
Suresh

Free to Be Me

Suhani Garg

I SILENTLY SNUCK DOWN THE STEPS, CRINGING AS I LANDED on a particularly squeaky one, hoping that my parents wouldn't hear. I reached the bottom and quickly pulled on my shoes and coat before quietly exiting the house.

I breathed a sigh of relief. I had managed to escape the house without getting caught! If my parents knew I had gone out without a hijab, they would probably send me off to Afghanistan to live with my strict grandmother. That was the last thing I wanted. But I shook my head and told myself, 'Tonight is your night! You are going to go out and enjoy yourself without any worries. For just one night, you are going to be a regular teenager.'

Then, I unchained my cycle and rode to my best friend Zi's house. She opened the door and immediately pulled me in, excitedly chatting about all the fun we were going to have. I nodded and smiled, but my mind was elsewhere – worrying about what I would do if I was caught. But then I decided that if I was caught and sent back to Afghanistan, then the night better be worth it. I was going to make this the best night of my life.

Zi was rummaging through her closet for a suitable outfit for me. All I had were neutral-coloured loose dresses, as I was not allowed to wear anything else. She pulled out a shiny black shirt and a pair of jeans for me, and, as I put them on, I could almost hear my dad talking about how inappropriate these were and what I should be wearing instead.

But I put on the clothes anyway and sat there with a smile as Zi curled my hair and applied makeup on me.

When she was finished, we got into her car and she drove us to a club. I asked her how we were going to get in as we were only seventeen, and she just winked and flashed a pair of fake IDs. We got in without a problem and, as soon as I entered, I was shocked. There were so many people! The loud music and smell of sweat and alcohol added to the infectious energy of freedom and fun.

Zi pulled me to the bar to get drinks for us. She was immediately swept away by a messy-haired boy as I sat there with both our drinks. I sat there for a while, simply observing everyone until Zi came back and pulled me onto the dance floor. We danced and drank for a couple of hours, having the time of our lives when suddenly, I heard my phone ringing.

I saw my father's name on the screen and froze. How did he find out I was out of the house?! I declined the call and forcefully pulled Zi out of the club, despite her protests. As soon as I uttered the word 'Dad', Zi was instantly alert. She drove us back to her house as fast as she could.

I quickly changed into my old clothes and removed my makeup. I couldn't do anything about my hair or the smell of alcohol on me, so I simply tied a scarf around my head as a makeshift hijab and sprayed on some perfume. I thanked Zi before grabbing my cycle and riding home as fast as I dared.

I had just barely entered when I heard my father's voice screaming at me to come into the living room. The moment I entered, I regretted my decision to go out. The look on my father's face was fearsome. He was boiling with rage, pacing up and down the room in his nightgown. My mother was perched on one of the armchairs, looking extremely frail and delicate next to my father's hulking figure.

'WHERE HAVE YOU BEEN?! HOW COULD YOU GO OUT IN THE MIDDLE OF THE NIGHT LIKE THAT?! When I first got Mr Shaan's call, I was shocked! And the clothes you were wearing; disgraceful! How could you do that? How could you bring shame to your family like that?' He was seething with anger.

'I'm sorry! I'm so, so sorry, Abba! I was just at Zi's house, and I was wearing just these clothes. Nothing else, I swear!' I plead with him.

'You're lying! Mr Shaan saw you in that disgusting club, wearing those horrible clothes that American teenagers wear. He told me they were black and tight! *Tight!* You cannot wear such clothes! No good Muslim girl would ever wear those kinds of clothes! You have greatly embarrassed us tonight.'

'I—I'm so sorry. I never meant to cause any harm. I'm sorry.'

'No, sorry doesn't cut it. You have to bear the consequences of this kind of behaviour.' With that, he grabbed one of the pokers sitting next to the fireplace.

I cringe knowing what was coming next. He draws his hand back before thrusting the poker at me with such force that I double over in pain as it strikes my arm. He draws his hand back for another swing and I bring my hands up to shield my face, but the hit doesn't come.

I see that my mother has grabbed his arm and is speaking to him in rapid Arabic, trying to reason with him. However, he simply flings her aside, causing her to hit her leg on the coffee table and fall onto the couch. He then hits me again, the blow landing on my stomach this time.

I can feel the sting of skin breaking and the wound beginning to bleed. I fall to the floor and curl up into a tight ball, my eyes filling with tears. My father seems satisfied as he puts the poker back in its place and steps over me to go to his room.

My mother gets up and comes over to me, examining the wounds before helping me to the kitchen, where the first-aid kit is kept. She cleans and bandages the wounds in silence, before kissing me on the forehead and going back to her room. I sit there, head on my knees, sobbing. After a bit, I get up and wipe my tears with the back of my hand.

I decided then that I can't continue living like this and rush to my room to pack a bag. I only carry some clothes and a picture of my family. I grab the bag, haul it outside and, with it on my shoulder, I slowly make my way to Zi's house.

The second Zi opens the door and sees me with a bag, tears streaming down my face and she pulls me into a tight hug. She tells me that I can stay at her house for as long as I want to. I thank her and we go up to her room where she sets up an air mattress as a makeshift bed for me.

The next morning, I wake up to see that I have ten missed calls and about a hundred messages from my father, demanding to know where I was. I switch off my phone and get ready for school. Halfway through the day, I am called to the principal's office and told that my parents are looking for me.

'You need to go home immediately,' they tell me.

I refuse and am sent to the guidance counsellor's office.

As soon as I enter the room, I can tell that she is extremely confused by the situation. 'Why don't you want to go home, Amira?' She sounds concerned.

'I don't want to go home because I want to truly live, Mrs Duvall. My whole life has been dictated by my parents and I have had absolutely zero say!'

I can see that this is all quite alien for her, so I plough on. 'I'll be turning eighteen very soon and then, a respectable suitor will be found for me. I will be forced to marry him and move to Afghanistan! All I wanted was one night out before that. But I wasn't allowed to have even that and so I ran away.'

I don't hear a response and look up to see a single tear rolling down her cheek.

'I am so sorry you have to have a life like that. But they are your legal guardians until you are eighteen and the school is legally required to tell them your whereabouts.' She shakes her head and sounds apologetic.

I beg her, 'Please, Mrs Duvall. Just one week!'

She relents, 'Fine. In five minutes, I will have to call to inform your parents about whether or not you're in school. If you can get out of the school by then, I will not know where you are and so will not be able to tell your parents either.'

I smile and say softly, 'Thank you so much. Just for one week, I promise.'

The days pass by with me going nowhere, but to Zi's house and to school, with Zi covering for me at home and Mrs Duvall at school. Four days later, I am suddenly called to the office in the middle of my lesson. As soon as I reach there, Mrs Duvall tells me my father has had a heart attack and I need to go home immediately.

I rush home as fast as I can only to see an ambulance taking my father away, his body covered with a white sheet. I stand there, stunned, tears rolling down my cheeks until I hear a cry and my mother runs over to me, hugging me, sobs wracking her body. I hug her back and we cry together as the ambulance takes his body away. The next few days pass quickly, with a flurry of visitors offering condolences as my mother and I stay in the house – unmoving, grieving.

The fourth day after the incident, my mother decides to finally get things in order. My father used to work in a small insurance firm and earned enough to support us, but there weren't enough savings to carry on for long after his death. My mother and I had a talk where we decided that instead of going back to Afghanistan, we would move to a smaller town. She could find a job there to support us.

We spend the week saying goodbye to all our friends, selling half of our possessions and finding a realtor to sell our house.

Exactly a week later, we are on the way to a town a couple of hours away from the city, in search of a new life. Though the road here was not easy, this is a new chapter in our lives – a huge change, hopefully for the better. I know that as long as I have my mother by my side, we can get through our grief and create a new life for ourselves.

And I'm looking forward to it.

Ammaji

Megha Mehta

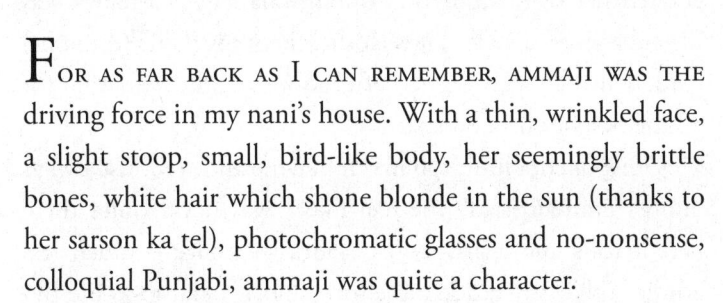

For as far back as I can remember, ammaji was the driving force in my nani's house. With a thin, wrinkled face, a slight stoop, small, bird-like body, her seemingly brittle bones, white hair which shone blonde in the sun (thanks to her sarson ka tel), photochromatic glasses and no-nonsense, colloquial Punjabi, ammaji was quite a character.

Growing up, she was, by turns, my favourite storyteller, playmate, confidante and nemesis. Our most epic fights were always around the same subject – my tendency to bury my nose in a book, rather than trying to learn all the 'essentials' (read: Cooking, stitching, knitting, et al).

'*Jal gayian twadiyan book-an*,' she would screech, cursing all my books to burn. Of course, I had a temper to match hers, and once, in a particularly nasty mood (she had snatched away my Wodehouse, so I could learn to crochet), got back with a '*Tussi te padhde likhde nahi ho, mainu te padhan dyu*'. It wasn't my finest moment, for girls in her time weren't even allowed to be educated.

This was one of the few occasions when she didn't get her way, and my self-righteous sulk carried me through the day.

Our other favourite subject to fight about was my weight. She would go on and on about how I should do jhaadu poocha '*paban bhar*', or squatting, and it would be my turn to tell her to mind her own weight. Which, of course, was never a problem – she was the most active person I knew. She usually cooked her own meals (her doodhwala gajar ka halwa was legendary), washed her own clothes, kept my nani's (dubious) garden alive, which was the afternoon langar destination for all the neighbourhood strays.

Outspoken, blunt, too much like me and, yet, just always 'more', ammaji made me feel like I was never quite there yet. It took me nearly two decades to realize – much less admit – that my academic efforts and general grab-life-by-the-horns attitude was as much a proverbial middle finger to her criticisms, as it was a reflection of her legacy.

No matter how our day went, or what stand-offs occurred between us (the rest of the family knew better than to interfere or try to reason with us), evenings always found me upstairs in her room, listening to her stories and telling her about my life over a glass of Bournvita – the milk heated to just the right degree and the Bournvita powder stirred endlessly till it was dissolved just so.

Some days, I would describe the book I was reading, some days she would describe the brand-new sparrow which had taken to feeding in her balcony, but our disagreements were banished to the graveyard of familial hurts and insults.

Sometimes, she would talk about life in Pakistan, in her beloved Pindi. But these occasions were few and far between, and when she did talk about her life, it sounded like she was narrating a fairy tale – beautiful, colourful, happy stories, but dreamy and otherworldly. They felt like they had no place in our reality. Only in our twilights – the moments between wakefulness and sleep.

One such hot (is there any other sort?) summer evening, we all dutifully trooped upstairs to the terrace. We were in for another eight-hour power outage, and just the thought of staying in the stuffy, steamy rooms downstairs was unbearable. It was the last summer I was able to spend a big chunk of time at my nani's. Life was changing. I had gotten admission to a prestigious engineering course and the long summer vacations I had enjoyed until now would soon be a distant memory.

The person most pleased by my admission was, unsurprisingly, ammaji. Not only because I was her beloved (and first!) great-grandchild, but also because I was to be an engineer. Her husband, after all, used to be an 'overseer' with the British government – the closest thing to an engineer in those days. Bauji later resigned from his job to set up a successful business, but ammaji never forgot that she was married to the most educated man in the Pind.

So upstairs it was, with buckets of water poured on the concrete floor to cool it down, our chataais sprinkled with rose water and rolled out on the floor. Ammaji and I settled down with our heads together, comfortable in our daily ritual of recapping our day. Maybe it was the upcoming change, the starry night on the terrace or the exceptional dahi wada we had for dinner, but our stories were mellow that night and the fairy tale seemed to slide right in.

***

Pindi, 1938

Kaushalya sat by her opulent dressing table (A dressing table! Who would have thought of such a thing!), going through her earrings to pick a pair. '*Paiyaji aande honge, pabi!*' her youngest nanad poked her head in the room and whispered, indicating to her sister-in-law that her husband had come home.

Kaushalya bent her head and nodded. The degree of laaj in the nod must've been satisfactory – she heard Paro giggle and run downstairs to convey the response to Kaushalya's saas.

Sighing, she picked the earrings for the night and proceeded to brush her hair – it wouldn't do to be anything less than presentable when she went down to help serve the evening meal.

As the newlywed daughter-in-law of one of the most respected families in Pindi, she wasn't to help with anything more than that around the house just yet. Her henna had started to fade, but it had been only seven days since her marriage.

'I won't let her in the kitchen for a full thirty days,' her saas had proudly proclaimed at her munhdikhai. And why not? Her saas had handpicked her for her beloved elder son, after all!

Kaushalya paused with the surma on her fingertip, leaning in to get a closer look at herself. She was the ugliest of her seven siblings – all of them tall, well-built, fair and smooth-featured. The 'ugly' had never bothered her; she knew she looked like her father – the colour of khameera aata (sourdough), with sharp features and an angular, thin frame.

Evidently, it didn't bother her saas either and, so far, her husband hadn't commented on her 'peculiar' appearance either. He had just been overjoyed to hear that she could read Urdu and manage to write a bit, too!

'Well, time to get going. Can't be late for the evening meal,' she thought, adjusting her ghoonghat as she walked downstairs.

***

Pindi, 1940

At the sound of the sniffle, Kaushalya froze! Waiting for her dadi saas to wake up and catch sight of 'Kaali Kaushi'.

'Here she goes ...' she thought and mentally prepared herself for the string of recriminations and creative taanas on her upbringing and family. But vaddi bebe simply turned over, let out a fart and went back to her snoring.

Swallowing her giggles with difficulty, Kaushalya wrapped the masala gud in her pallu and eased through the door to meet Paro, who had been standing guard just outside the door. As they ran to the safety of the terrace, the two burst out laughing – co-conspirators in a crime!

Kaushalya knew she would miss this nanad, her last link to her own childhood, when Paro got married in the winter. Paro had made the transition into a new house so much smoother for Kaushalya, and the past two years had just flown by.

Being the beloved youngest child, Paro had managed to delay her gauna till the ripe old age of sixteen. Only one year older than her, Kaushalya still felt vastly more grown up, especially now that she was a mother. Ved was the most adorable toddler, and her saas and paiyaji were pleased as punch.

'*Ek kudi jaan lagi hai te dooji aa gayi*,' her saas had exclaimed – one daughter might have been leaving the house, but another had come.

'Well, today, we have this freshly stolen gud.' Kaushalya turned to Paro. 'May your life be the same as this gud – sweet with an underlying spice!'

***

Pindi, 1945

As she stepped out of the rickshaw with her son, Kaushalya wished she could bounce in her excitement like he did … paiyaji had bought a second shop! They said it was at least three times bigger the current one … Just imagine!

Paro had pestered him endlessly to take them there and paiyaji had been unable to refuse his darling sister, Paro, home from her sasural for her first delivery. It had been a tough pregnancy, but, finally, after five years of marriage, Paro had carried a child through the first trimester.

Now in her sixth month, looking happy and healthy, she exclaimed, 'Look at the dukaan, pabi, the name is written in angrezi! How modern it is looking, and it is coloured blue! Oh, and paiyaji … He looks so handsome, so authoritative!'

'You can read angrezi?' Kaushalya asked her husband that night.

'Yes, of course, my bauji had arranged an English tutor when I was young. He wanted his sons to be able to speak the language of the sahibs.'

'I want to read your shop's board. Can you teach me?'

But how was that to happen? In a house of seventeen people, how would the eldest son and daughter-in-law ever have time to themselves?

One day, Kaushalya saw a book on her mantle.

'Book?' I interrupted ammaji's story. 'Aap books bhi padhte the? Mujhe to bada sunaate the meri book-an ko leke.' After everything she had said to me about my books, I couldn't believe she had read one.

'Paiyaji had bought it for me. It was a book of angrezi ABCD, and he put my name on the front page – Smt Kaushalya Devi. That's how I knew it was for me.'

'Phir?'

'Phir kya, beta? Tere chote nanaji aa gaye, phir Ved got married, my saas died, my devar shifted to Peshawar.' She laughed. 'Life happened.'

'And you lost the book?'

'Not right off. I packed it when we left Pindi to come to India, and then ...'

I knew what had happened after that. My great grandfather had died one day after they reached the refugee camp, when my nanaji was only eighteen years old, leaving ammaji a widow at thirty-eight. The vultures had descended and taken over the business and everything of value while the widow and her two sons struggled with their grief.

The erstwhile 'rani' now had to stitch clothes and do other odd jobs to scrape together money to survive. She begged her brothers for scraps, and survived most days on a meal of roti and pyaaz (even pickle was a delicacy for her and was only available sometimes as a result of people's charity). For the next decade of her life, till both her sons had settled and things stabilized, she worked her fingers to the bone.

In that moment between wakefulness and sleep, I saw an ammaji, who was not yet my ammaji. Just a girl like me …

***

Ammaji's funeral was the biggest family get-together I had ever seen – at least a third of the people attending were relatives I had never seen before! The next two days were full of laughter as we shared anecdotes about her – her ninety-eight years on this earth and her essential contrariness had supplied us with enough material.

As we went to Haridwar to immerse her ashes, the mimicry and recollections continued – the mood celebratory rather than funereal. I thought about the strays we had fed every day, the carefully hoarded dabba of Bournvita we found in ammaji's belongings, which she was saving for my next trip, her white saris being packed to be distributed to other widows …

Guruji's ashram was the last stop on our trip – we just needed to sign off the donations in ammaji's name and we would leave for Delhi that afternoon. I couldn't shake off the feeling that I was leaving her behind, this beloved friend of mine. I feared that I would forget her in the future and the best parts of my childhood.

I slipped out of the ashram and, wandering around the town, I found myself at a tiny shop crammed floor to ceiling with my favourite thing in the world. Book-an, as ammaji called them. Small-town bookstores are fascinating – some of the most eclectic and disparate bits and pieces are usually found there. This one in Rishikesh was no exception.

I picked up what looked to be an ancient children's English alphabet book, and started to flip through it. I broke out into goosebumps when I saw the inscription on the first page.

There, in faded ink, were a couple of words in Urdu!

I did not need to get the inscription translated, for the heart knows what it knows.

A Note from the Author

Every time I have launched a book, someone in the audience inevitably asks, 'Will you ever write fiction?'

And I would answer, 'No, there are so many real-life stories to tell.'

But then, Covid-19 happened and the world turned upside down. And, in a sense, so did I. On 15 April 2020, stuck at home, the world at a standstill, I wrote my first short fiction story. It felt good. Another idea popped into my mind; I wrote a second story.

Then I said to myself, 'Can I write a story a day for thirty days?'

My brain started buzzing. Each night I would tell myself, 'Give me an idea for tomorrow.' And I would actually wake up with one. I would then feverishly type out the story of the day and share it with a few friends. 'Give us more,' they said. 'Can we share this with other friends?'

This book is born out of that thirty-day challenge I set for myself. When I realized that fiction and non-fiction are two sides of the same coin. All the material comes from life.

My favourite short story writers are O. Henry and Jeffrey Archer. Hence, like them, I tried to give every story of mine 'a twist in the tale'.

As my thirty-day challenge drew to a close, I noticed that everything from yoga to gourmet cooking was being taught online. So why not writing? I devised a method of 'learning by doing', where, in a span of three short hours, participants could awaken the storyteller that lies in all of us.

In the past two and a half years, more than 500 students from all age groups and all walks of life have attended these workshops. And have written fabulous stories (some are included in this book!).

My foray into fiction has just begun. My dream is to be a screenwriter, churning out binge-worthy episodes on socially relevant subjects. People tell me, 'It's not going to be easy', and I agree. Nothing your soul longs for, ever is.

Challenge yourself with things you've never done before.

The power of imagination will open every door.

Acknowledgements

This book was made possible only because of the unstinting love and support I received from my housekeeper, Lata. While others struggled with ghar ka kaam, I was kept well-fed and well-rested by her. My fingers were flying on the keyboard and not ghisoing dishes. Unlike most during the lockdown.

Thank you to my dear colleague, Varsha, who quickly adjusted to the challenges of lockdown, as we pivoted our business from selling books to conducting workshops during that period. Her 'we shall overcome' attitude and cheerful smile kept me going on many a dull day.

My daughter, Nivedita, who tolerated me and my moods during the lockdown. And gave me the space I needed as a writer.

Yatin, for always being a support to us and to my parents, during this difficult time.

Surbhi Jain and Niket Agarwal for helping me set up a basic WordPress site to share my stories. What would I have done without you!

Aruna Raje, for sharpening my fiction-writing capacity with her amazing screenwriting workshops.

My primero friends, Bharati, Namrata and Rhea, for keeping me sane during the lockdown.

Our doggo, Maya, who loves me as only a crazy canine can.

The team at Harper Collins for believing in me as a fiction writer.

And my soul friend, Sharad, for encouraging me to step into 'Act 2'. I resisted, but I am slowly getting there!

Rashmi Bansal
December 2022
Mumbai

About the Authors

Rashmi Bansal is a writer, entrepreneur and motivational speaker. She is the author of ten bestselling books on entrepreneurship – *Stay Hungry, Stay Foolish, Connect the Dots, I Have a Dream, Poor Little Rich Slum, Follow Every Rainbow, Take Me Home, Arise, Awake, God's Own Kitchen, Touch the Sky* and *Shine Bright* – which have sold more than 12 lakh copies and been translated into twelve languages. She conducts online writing workshops and mentors students and young entrepreneurs. Rashmi is an economics graduate from Sophia College, Mumbai, and an MBA from IIM Ahmedabad. Visit https://rashmibansal.in/ and subscribe to get access to exclusive new stories every month.

About the Authors

Suhani Garg is a sixteen-year-old girl currently living in Bangalore. Her interests include reading, writing and art.

Devakee is a management consultant who lives in Mumbai with her furry and hairy family. She enjoys reading, writing slice-of-life stories, poetry and creating sustainable art.

Rengarajan is an MTech (Civil), IITM, PGDM (Finance) with three decades of experience in the Oil and Gas Industry. Now retired, he loves to read and write stories.

Srivatsan G. is a corporate finance professional with a flair for writing.

Marketeer by profession, storyteller by choice, **Megha** is excited to share the semi-autobiographical tale of her ammaji with readers.

Bhuvaneswari comes from Tamil Nadu and lives in Bangalore. She is a working professional with immense interest in reading and writing.

Learn the Art of Writing with Rashmi Bansal

(All workshops held on Zoom, on weekends)

Short-story Writing Workshop (twice a month)

If you want to start telling your stories, register for this hands-on workshop. The goal is to have a complete story written by you at the end of just 3 hours.

Bonus: The best stories from the workshop get published on my website.

Deep-dive Non-fiction Workshop (2 days, once a month)

This workshop is designed for anyone who is keen on writing an impactful non-fiction book.

The workshop is practical in nature and features hands-on exercises as well as Q&A sessions.

I also cover 'how to get published' and provide a review for 3 chapters of your book.

Personal Storytelling Workshop (once a month)

Whether you are a CEO or a junior manager, stories will help you energize your team and build your personal brand. Learn how to tell your personal story with confidence and flair.

All workshop attendees also become part of a virtual writing community.

Want to conduct workshops for your school, college, institute, or for your team at your organization?
Write to us at enquiry@rashmibansal.in with your requirement.

For workshop dates visit: https://rashmibansal.in/workshops

30 Years *of*
HarperCollins *Publishers* India

At HarperCollins, we believe in telling the best stories and finding the widest possible readership for our books in every format possible. We started publishing 30 years ago; a great deal has changed since then, but what has remained constant is the passion with which our authors write their books, the love with which readers receive them, and the sheer joy and excitement that we as publishers feel in being a part of the publishing process.

Over the years, we've had the pleasure of publishing some of the finest writing from the subcontinent and around the world, and some of the biggest bestsellers in India's publishing history. Our books and authors have won a phenomenal range of awards, and we ourselves have been named Publisher of the Year the greatest number of times. But nothing has meant more to us than the fact that millions of people have read the books we published, and somewhere, a book of ours might have made a difference.

As we step into our fourth decade, we go back to that one word – a word which has been a driving force for us all these years.

Read.

Harper Collins | 4th | HARPER PERENNIAL | HARPER BUSINESS | HARPER BLACK | हार्पर हिन्दी

HarperCollins *Children'sBooks* | HARPER DESIGN | HARPER VANTAGE | Harper Sport